He smelled her before he saw her, that sweet pear scent that instantly aroused him.

She stood in the doorway of his room. "Maggie?" he said softly.

"I'm looking for a nice Southern gentleman named Jackson," she said, her voice slightly husky.

"That would be me," he replied, his chest suddenly tight with anticipation.

"I thought you might be interested in a night with a woman who isn't looking for anything more than this night and this night only."

"Maggie..." He said her name with hesitation. Man, he wanted her. He thought he might even need her. But he knew things she didn't know, things that would forever stand between them and make any future impossible.

SCENE OF THE CRIME: RETURN TO MYSTIC LAKE

New York Times Bestselling Author

CARLA CASSIDY

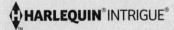

Recycling programs
for this product may
not exist in your area.

ISBN-13: 978-0-373-69761-8

SCENE OF THE CRIME: RETURN TO MYSTIC LAKE

Copyright © 2014 by Carla Bracale

This edition published by arrangement with Harlequin Books S.A.

For questions and comments about the quality of this book, please contact us at CustomerService@Harlequin.com.

Printed in U.S.A.

www.Harlequin.com

ABOUT THE AUTHOR

New York Times bestselling author Carla Cassidy is an award-winning author who has written more than fifty novels for Harlequin. In 1995, she won Best Silhouette Romance from *RT Book Reviews* for *Anything for Danny*. In 1998, she also won a Career Achievement Award for Best Innovative Series from *RT Book Reviews*.

Carla believes the only thing better than curling up with a good book to read is sitting down at the computer with a good story to write. She's looking forward to writing many more books and bringing hours of pleasure to readers.

Books by Carla Cassidy

CAST OF CHARACTERS

Jackson Revannaugh—Laid-back, smooth-talking FBI agent who loves the ladies almost as much as he loves solving crimes.

Marjorie Clinton—FBI agent. She's fiercely independent and feels an instant dislike and desire for her new partner, Jackson.

John Merriweather—The ex-husband of missing FBI agent Amberly Caldwell. Had he finally grown tired of sharing custody of their seven-year-old son, Max?

Edward Bentz—A man who has ties to Louisiana and Kansas City—does he have a connection to the kidnappings that have occurred in both locations?

Jeff Maynard—A bartender who hated Amberly and her new husband, Cole.

Natalie Redwing—Was she stalking Amberly's husband before the couple disappeared?

Jimmy Tanner—Good friends with Jeff Maynard. Was he a coconspirator in the crime that had taken place in the small town of Mystic Lake?

Chapter One

Jackson Revannaugh knew he was in the land of Oz when the jet touched down in the middle of a patchwork of farmers' fields. Nowhere near the Kansas City International Airport did he see any signs of a city.

It was already after 7:00 p.m. and he was eager to get off the plane. The flight from Baton Rouge had been over three hours long, and not only had a baby cried the entire trip, but the kid behind him had seemed to find great amusement in kicking the back of Jackson's seat at regular intervals.

Jackson was working up to a stellar foul mood. Too little sleep in the past couple weeks, a long ride in cramped quarters and a bag of pretzels as his only food for the past eight hours or so had made Jackson a cranky man.

Thankfully, it took him only minutes to deplane. From the overhead bin he grabbed the large duffel bag that held everything he would need for the duration of his stay in Kansas City, Missouri. He then headed down the walkway toward the terminal entrance.

Just ahead of him were double doors that led outside the building. As he exited, Jackson realized that the humid mid-July heat of the Midwest had nothing on

Bachelor Moon, Louisiana, where he'd spent the past several weeks of his life working on the case of a missing man, his wife and his seven-year-old stepdaughter.

He'd been yanked from that case before they'd had any answers and sent directly here to work on something similar. He stepped to the edge of the curb and fought the exhaustion that, over the past month, had settled on his shoulders like a heavy weight.

He'd been told a car would pick him up to take him to the small town of Mystic Lake, a thirty-minute drive from Kansas City. But he hadn't been told specifically what kind of a car to look for.

What he'd like right about now was a big, juicy steak, a tall glass of bourbon, a ride to the nearest posh hotel for fluffy bath towels, a king-size bed and about twelve hours of uninterrupted sleep.

Instead he stepped to the curb with a frown and the knowledge that it was probably going to be a long night and he wasn't at the top of his game.

He had been given no details about whatever crime had taken place here; he knew only that he was to work with a partner from the Kansas City FBI field office.

Now if he could just find his ride, he could, sooner rather than later, solve the crime and be on his way back out of town and home to his luxury apartment in Baton Rouge.

He stepped back from the curb as a large blue bus pulled to the curb and belched a whoosh of hot exhaust. The doors swung open and for a brief moment Jackson wondered if he was supposed to get on the bus, but that didn't make any sense.

When he'd spoken briefly on the phone earlier to Director Daniel Forbes of the Kansas City field office, he'd told Jackson to stand on the curb outside the luggage area of Terminal A and a car would be waiting.

He remained standing, tamping down an edge of new irritation. Where was the car? His plane had been right on time.

When the bus finally pulled away, a black sedan slid next to the curb. A petite woman with shoulder-length strawberry-blond curls and eyes the green of a Louisiana swamp opened the driver door and stood.

If there was one thing that could transform Jackson from a grouch to a gentleman, it was the sight of an attractive woman. God, he loved women.

"Agent Revannaugh?" she asked.

"That would be me," he replied. He opened the back door and tossed his duffel bag onto the seat and then got into the passenger seat.

She got back behind the steering wheel, bringing with her the scent of honeysuckle and spice. Clad in a pair of tight black slacks and a short-sleeved white blouse that hugged her breasts and emphasized a slender waist, she was definitely a hum of pleasure in Jackson's overworked brain.

As she swept her hair behind one ear, he noted what appeared to be a nice-sized emerald earring. Emeralds were a good choice for her, with her green eyes.

"Well, I feel my mood lifting already," he said as she pulled away from the curb and into the traffic lane that would take them away from the airport terminal. "Darlin', I wasn't expecting my driver to be such a gorgeous piece of eye candy. What a nice welcome to Kansas City." As usual when Jackson worked his charm, his Southern accent grew thicker and more distinct.

She slid him a quick, cool glance and then focused back on the road. "You just assume I'm nothing but your driver because I'm a woman? Hmm, not only a silly flirt, but a chauvinist, as well," she replied. "I haven't had a chance to introduce myself yet. I'm Special Agent Marjorie Clinton, lead investigator on this case. You'll be working with me and you'll quickly discover I'm not anyone's 'darlin.'"

Jackson sat up straighter in his chair, seeking a mental shovel to get out of the hole he'd already dug for himself. "I'm not a chauvinist," he finally said. "I was told a driver would pick me up—I just assumed you were my driver and nothing more. And you might not be anyone's darlin', but you're definitely a fine piece of eye candy."

He watched her slender, ringless fingers tighten on the steering wheel and realized he'd just made the hole a little bigger. "Since it appears we're going to be partners, perhaps it would be nice if we start all over again. Hello, I'm Special Agent Jackson Revannaugh."

Once again those lush green eyes slid in his direction and then back to the road. "We're about twenty minutes from Mystic Lake, a small town on the outskirts of Kansas City. I suggest we use that twenty minutes with me filling you in on things rather than pretending to play nice together. How much do you know about the case?"

"Virtually nothing," Jackson admitted. She might look like a hot piece of work, but there was nothing hot in the cool disdain in her eyes when she glanced at him. *Focus on the work and then get the heck out of Dodge,* he thought.

"I was pulled off a case I was working in Bachelor

Moon, Louisiana, and instantly dispatched here with no details other than the fact that this case appears to have some similarity to the one I was working."

"Missing persons?" She turned off a four-lane highway and onto a two-lane that appeared to take them farther away from civilization.

"Three people seemingly disappeared into thin air at some point during an evening. Evidence of an interrupted late-night snack was on the table, but the two adults and one child have yet to be found. Me and a couple of my partners were on the case for several weeks and we found no clues, no real leads to follow."

He took the opportunity to study her. Faint freckles, evident in the fading light of day, smattered the bridge of her nose. He had a feeling she wasn't a woman who smiled often, although he knew instinctively that a smile would light up her face, warm her features into something even more beautiful.

"We have two missing persons, but unfortunately we don't have a specific time line as to when exactly they went missing. The couple, Amberly Caldwell and her husband, Cole, were newlyweds, and were transitioning between Cole's house in Mystic Lake and Amberly's home in Kansas City."

She stopped talking and slowed to make a right-hand turn, and then continued. "Amberly has a son, Max. The boy had spent the weekend with his father, John Merriweather. The arrangement was that Amberly would pick up Max from school yesterday afternoon. When she didn't show up, John got worried and drove to Cole's place."

"But they weren't there."

Marjorie gave a curt nod of her head. "Both of their

cars were in the driveway, but he couldn't rouse them. Unfortunately, the deputy who had been called out made the determination that it would be best to give it twenty-four hours before officially doing anything."

"He didn't do a well-check?" Jackson asked in surprise. A well-check would have required an officer to get inside the house to make certain the occupants were okay.

"Small police force, underzealous officers and two people who aren't old or sick." Her voice once again held a faint touch of derision. "It was only late this afternoon that an officer finally broke into the front door and discovered that things weren't right inside. That's when my director got a phone call from Roger Black, Mystic Lake's number one deputy. Apparently our director knew what was going on in Louisiana, and that's when you were dispatched here."

"I've heard there's nothing better than Kansas City steaks, and my first impression of the women of the city is definitely a positive one." He couldn't help himself. Part of the way he prepared himself, part of his process in approaching a crime, was to small talk, to attempt to get on the good side of whoever he'd be working with during the course of an investigation.

Marjorie shot him a baleful look. Apparently she didn't have a good side, he thought, as he sighed and stared out the passenger window, where the landscape was so different from what he was accustomed to.

Here there were stately oaks and leafy maples, stretches of fields with cornstalks reaching high. There were no graceful magnolia trees or cypresses with Spanish moss hanging like ghostly spiderwebs.

Jackson had never been out of Louisiana before.

Kansas City would have to work hard to match the beauty and charm of his home state.

Speaking of charm, he turned his head to look at Marjorie. "Have you already been to the scene?"

"I came from there to pick you up," she replied. "We've just done a cursory walk-through of the house. The crime scene unit hasn't touched it. Nobody else has been inside except me and a couple of the Mystic Lake deputies. We were waiting for the hotshot from Louisiana to officially begin."

"And that would be me," he replied easily. "So, what did the initial walk-through tell you?"

"I'd rather you draw your own conclusions by seeing it first. I can tell you this—the doors were all locked and there is no sign of forced entry anywhere."

"Tell me more about the potential victims. Who they are and what they do." A victim rundown was usually as helpful as an official profile of the potential perpetrator.

"Cole Caldwell, thirty-six years old. He and Amberly married less than two months ago. She's thirty-one, has a seven-year-old son and is a beautiful Native American woman. Apparently the two of them had been spending weekends packing up Caldwell's place and getting his house ready to put on the market, as they'd decided to live full-time in Amberly's home in Kansas City."

Her voice was pleasant, but her tone was all business. "Amberly shares custody of Max with her exhusband, who lives down the block from her house. They had an arrangement that worked well for everyone involved."

"You never told me what each of them does for a living," Jackson asked.

"Cole Caldwell is the sheriff of Mystic Lake." She turned into the driveway of an attractive ranch house where several other Mystic Lake patrol cars were parked. She pulled up next to the curb, cut the engine and then turned to face Jackson.

For the first time a hint of emotion darkened her green eyes. "Amberly works with me. She is one of the brightest FBI profilers in the area."

Jackson's stomach gave an unpleasant lurch. "That's odd. The case I was investigating in Bachelor Moon involved a man named Sam Connelly, a retired FBI profiler from the Kansas City office."

MARJORIE HAD BEEN SICK from the moment she'd realized that one of the missing persons was Amberly. Although the two women hadn't been superclose friends and had never worked a case together, they'd been friendly. Everyone in the office was on edge due to this new development.

She was grateful to get out of the car, where the scent of Jackson Revannaugh's cologne had been far too pleasant. It whispered of bold maleness and an exotic spiciness that could be intoxicating if allowed.

She didn't like him. She knew his type…the hotshot Southern charmer who never met a woman he wouldn't take advantage of, who skated through life on a lazy smile and smooth style.

Oh, yes, she knew his type intimately, and she wasn't about to fall prey to his questionable charisma. All she wanted was for the two of them to work as hard as possible to get Amberly and Cole back where they belonged.

Deputy Fred Morsi stood at the door as sentry. "Nobody has been inside since you left," he said to Marjorie, as if assuring her he'd done his job properly.

He was one of the first locals Marjorie had met when she'd arrived on scene, and he'd instantly impressed her with his earnest face and professional attitude.

Marjorie nodded and grabbed a pair of booties from a box sitting on the front porch. As she pulled them on over her black sneakers, she noticed Jackson doing the same over his expensive-looking leather shoes. He grabbed a pair of latex gloves, his easy smile gone and his mouth set in a grim line instead.

So, there was another side to the hot Mr. Southern Charm, she thought. She frowned as she realized she'd just thought of Jackson Revannaugh as hot.

Of course, she was certain most women would find him a hunk, with his slightly long, slightly curly black hair and blue eyes, with chiseled features and a mouth that looked soft and pliable. She stifled a yelp as the latex of her glove snapped her wrist.

"Shall we?" she said to the tall, broad-shouldered man who was her temporary partner. She gestured to the closed front door.

"After you, darlin'," he replied, and then winced. "I didn't mean that…. Force of habit."

The front door opened into a small formal living room. The only pieces of furniture were a couple of end tables and a stack of large boxes. Jackson stopped just inside the door behind Marjorie.

His dark blue eyes narrowed and he lifted his

head, like a wild animal sniffing the air for prey. "No evidence that anything happened in this room?"

"Nothing," she replied. The small formal living room opened into a large great-room/kitchen area. Here was the evidence that something unusual had taken place.

She followed Jackson's gaze as it traveled around the room, taking in the oversize pillows on the floor in front of a coffee table that held two half-empty wineglasses and a platter of hardened, too-yellow cheddar cheese, crackers, and grapes starting to wither and emanate a slightly spoiled scent.

Jackson picked up one of the long-stem glasses and sniffed the contents. "Fruity... I smell a touch of cherry and plum and a faint dash of damp leather. Pinot noir would be my guess." He set the glass back on the table as Marjorie stared at him in astonishment.

"There's a bottle of pinot noir open on the kitchen counter," she replied in surprise.

Jackson nodded. "Like a good Southern gentleman, I know my wines, although I definitely prefer a good glass of bourbon or brandy, and preferably with a lovely lady by my side."

"But, of course," she replied dryly.

He frowned at the coffee table. "So, it appears our two missing souls were seated here sharing what appears to be cocktail time together."

"And something happened to interrupt their intimate little party," Marjorie said.

"So it seems." Jackson turned away from the coffee table and his gaze swept around the room. "No sign of a struggle. What have we here?" Nearly hidden at the edge of one of the pillows was a small black purse.

He opened it and pulled out a cell phone, a wallet and a tube of lipstick.

Marjorie's heart tumbled a little lower in her chest as she watched him open up the slender wallet. Inside was Amberly's identification, thirty-two dollars and two credit cards.

"If somebody came in here to confront the two, it wasn't anybody with robbery on their mind," he said, his voice that low Southern drawl that Marjorie found both irritating and evocatively inviting at the same time.

He placed the items back in the purse. "We'll take that phone to your techies at the bureau and see if they can find anything useful. Maybe somebody called and the two of them rushed out of here on an emergency."

"Amberly would have let John know," Marjorie replied with conviction.

He walked from the coffee table toward the kitchen area, his footsteps surprisingly heavy for a man who appeared so physically fit and agile.

She followed him into the kitchen, where she knew he would find nothing suspicious, nothing that might indicate what exactly had happened to Cole and Amberly.

She leaned a slender hip against the cabinet and watched as he checked the back door, opened drawers and cabinets that were mostly empty. He pulled a small notepad and pen from the pocket of his pristine white shirt and took some notes.

He might be an arrogant, smooth-talking pain in her butt, but he also appeared to be thorough and detail driven, and that was the only thing important to her in this case. Nothing else mattered, as long as he was as good at his job as he looked in his expensive white shirt and the tailored black slacks that fit him to perfection. He wore his gun and holster on a sleek leather belt around his waist, looking both lethal and sexy at the same time.

From the minute she had joined the FBI, nothing had mattered but the job and caretaking for her mother. This particular case hit too close to home, with a fellow FBI agent gone missing.

"Let's take a look at the rest of the house," he finally said when he'd finished checking out the kitchen.

"There isn't much here. Two bedrooms have already been emptied of all the furniture, and there's just a bed and a dresser left in the master suite."

His footsteps thundered down the hallway, and he peeked into each room as they passed, finally stopping just inside the master bedroom.

"Smart man," he said as he gazed at the bed with the navy bedspread. "He's moved most of the furniture out but left a spot for foreplay in the family room and the bed to complete the night." He turned to look at Marjorie and she was horrified to feel a warmth steal into her cheeks. Thank goodness he didn't mention it.

"So, Amberly and Cole came here Friday night to pack things away, and Monday afternoon she didn't show up to pick up her kid from school," he continued. "Do you know if anyone spoke to either of them between those times?" he asked.

"When I left here to pick you up at the airport I had a couple of deputies and another FBI agent canvassing the neighborhood to find out the last time either of them was seen."

She pulled her cell phone out of her pocket and

punched in a number. "Adam. Any news?" She listened to the report, acutely aware of Jackson's gaze taking her in from head to toe.

The temperature inside the house was a comfortable one for the heat of the night, but as her new partner's gaze slid down the length of her, she felt the atmosphere in the room climb at least ten degrees warmer.

"Thanks," she said to FBI agent Adam Forest, and then hung up. "According to what the officers have been able to find out for now, the next-door neighbor, Charles Baker, saw Cole and Amberly arrive here just after five on Friday night. About seven that same night he saw Cole again when he mowed the lawn. Nobody saw either of them after that...at least that we've talked to so far."

She watched him open the top drawer of the dresser. She hadn't had a chance to check things out this thoroughly before leaving the scene earlier to pick him up at the airport.

"Unless Sheriff Cole Caldwell is an unusual man for a sheriff, he didn't leave here of his own volition." He pulled a handgun from the drawer, along with a gold badge. "No sheriff I know would take off without his weapon and the very thing that defines him."

Every muscle in Marjorie's body tensed at the sight of the items. She'd hoped that this was all some kind of a mistake, that little Max and his father had somehow misunderstood, and Cole and Amberly had gone off for a mini-honeymoon.

"So, is this like what you were working on in Bachelor Moon?" she asked Jackson.

"Too early for me to make that jump." He left the

bedroom and she hurried after him. He walked back into the great room and stared at the coffee table and the oversize pillows. "On the surface things look very similar to what I was working on in Bachelor Moon, but it would be a mistake for us to leap to any conclusions this early in the investigation."

"I can take you to Amberly's place now. I have a couple of officers sitting on it so that nothing is disturbed."

Together they stepped outside, where they both removed their booties and gloves. "I'll be honest with you—at the moment what I need is a good meal, a strong drink and a soft bed," Jackson said.

"But we still need to go to Amberly's," Marjorie protested.

"That can wait until morning," Jackson said. "Whatever happened to Sheriff Caldwell and his wife happened here, not at the house in Kansas City. We've got a lot of work ahead of us."

"Exactly," Marjorie replied. "And we need to work through the night if that's what it takes to get to the bottom of this."

"It's going to take more than a single night to get to the bottom of this," Jackson said as he headed for her car.

She hurried after him, irritated by his lack of work ethic. She didn't know how they solved crime in Louisiana, but they sure as heck didn't do it in Kansas City by eating a good steak and finding a soft bed.

"But you know how important the first forty-eight hours are right after a crime," she said as they got into her car.

"I know, but as far as I can figure, we've already

lost our first forty-eight-hour window. My gut says they disappeared from here sometime Friday night, and here we are on Tuesday night. Besides, at this point all we have is two people not where they said they would be…nothing to indicate that an actual crime took place at all."

"Trust me, if Amberly told Max she'd pick him up at school yesterday, nothing would have kept her away except something terrible," Marjorie replied. "Max always came first with her."

"Have you checked the local hospitals? Maybe one of them got sick and hasn't had a chance to call." He obviously read on her face that it hadn't been done yet.

"Then that's something you can take care of after you drop me off at whatever place I'm staying while I'm here in town."

"You aren't staying here in Mystic Lake. The director set you up in a motel in Kansas City. Don't worry, there's a restaurant right next door where you can feed your face." She started the engine, fighting a new blast of irritation directed at him.

FBI agents didn't work normal business hours. When in the middle of a case they worked until they physically couldn't work any longer.

To make matters worse, as she began the drive back toward the city, not only did Special Agent Jackson Revannaugh fall asleep, but the car filled with his faint, deep snores.

She was livid that she'd put off beginning the official investigation until this Louisiana man had arrived. She was ticked off that somehow her director thought he could potentially add a valuable perspective on the crime.

As if fate hadn't already delivered enough painful hits in her life, it had now delivered up to her the partner from hell.

Chapter Two

Jackson shot straight up in bed, his heart beating frantically as early-morning light shone through the half-closed curtains on the nearby window. It took him several minutes to process the nightmares that had haunted his sleep and a little more time to realize exactly where he was.

Kansas City…the Regent Motel. He muttered a curse as he saw the time. Six-thirty, and if he remembered right, Agent Uptight's last words to him after dropping him off the night before were that she'd be here to pick him up at seven.

Coffee. He needed coffee to take away the lingering taste of the nightmares that had chased through his sleep. He spied a small coffeemaker on the vanity and waited for it to brew the single cup. While the coffee was brewing, he unlocked his motel room door just in case Marjorie showed up early.

Once the coffee was ready, he took a big swallow and then carried the cup into the bathroom and set it on the counter while he got into the shower.

He knew Marjorie was angry that he had called a halt to the night before, but he'd also known that he wouldn't be any real asset to her unless he took the night to catch up on some sleep. The case in Bachelor Moon had nearly drained him dry, both physically and mentally, and he'd needed last night to transition, to prepare himself for this new investigation.

At least she'd been right—while the motel wasn't five stars, it was adequate and there was a decent restaurant next door. He'd walked there last night and had enjoyed his first taste of Kansas City barbecue... a pulled-pork sandwich and the best onion rings he'd ever tasted.

Maybe it was the sweet, tangy sauce that had given him the nightmares, he thought as he turned off the water and stepped out of the enclosure.

His dreams had been haunted by Sam Connelly, his wife, Daniella, and their little girl, Macy—the missing family from Bachelor Moon, who had yet to be found. Dashing around the edges of the darkness had been two more figures who he knew in his dream were Cole Caldwell and his wife, Amberly. And then there had been his father.

Jerrod Revannaugh had no place in his dreams, just as he had no place in Jackson's life. The bond between father and son had been fractured long ago and finally completely broken just a little over five years ago.

He shoved away any lingering thoughts of nightmares, especially images of the man who had raised him, and instead wrapped a towel around his waist and got out his shaving kit.

Jackson knew he was a handsome man. It wasn't anything he thought much about, just a fact he saw when he looked in a mirror. He was simply the product of good genes.

He also knew he had a charm about him that drew

women to him, and though he enjoyed an occasional liaison with a sophisticated woman who knew the score, he made certain they also knew he was merely after a brief encounter and not interested in matters of the heart.

He was definitely not his father's son. He might look like Jerrod Revannaugh, and the two men might share the Revannaugh ability to charm, but Jackson would never be the coldhearted bastard that his father had been. He always made sure his partner knew the score, unlike his father who had spent his life taking advantage of naïve women.

While he found his new partner hot to look at, she had a prickly exterior that he had no interest in digging beneath. Besides, it wasn't as if he anticipated Agent Marjorie Clinton jumping his bones. She'd made it fairly clear that she didn't particularly like him and would tolerate him only in order to further the investigation.

He'd managed to razor off the shaving cream on half of his face when he heard a firm knock on his door. A glance at the clock by the nightstand showed him it was ten until seven. He knew she was the type to be early.

"Come on in," he shouted, and heard the door open. He leaned out of the bathroom to see her standing just inside the door. "You're early."

She shot ramrod straight. Her eyes widened and then her gaze instantly dropped to the carpeting, as if unable to look at him. "And it appears that you're going to be late. I'll just wait for you out in the car."

She ran out of the room like a rabbit being chased by a hound dog and slammed the door behind her.

Jackson turned back to the mirror in amusement. He hadn't exactly been naked, but she'd skedaddled out of the room like a virgin.

He quickly finished his shaving, slapped on some cologne, grabbed his white shirt and slacks—neatly pressed the night before and on hangers—and dressed.

He had a feeling the longer she sat in the car waiting for him, the more difficult the mood would be between them. He suspected it was already going to be a long day. Her being cranky with him would only make it longer.

It was exactly three minutes after seven when he slid into the passenger seat of her car and shut the door. "Sorry I'm late. The last thing I would ever want to do is keep a lovely lady waiting," he said with a smile.

"Stuff it, Rhett. I'm uncharmable and you might as well stop trying." She started the car and pulled out of the parking space in front of his unit.

"Why, Scarlett, I haven't even begun to attempt to charm you yet," he replied with his trademark lazy grin.

She frowned. "We have a busy day ahead. We checked all the hospitals last night both here in Kansas City and in Mystic Lake. Cole and Amberly aren't in any of them. I've set up an interview with John Merriweather, Amberly's ex-husband, after nine. He didn't want us at his place until after Max had left for school. I've also directed a couple of agents to check what cases Amberly was working on, and the same with Cole. There are also some other people we need to interview before the day is done. I have a list in my briefcase."

"Wow, you've been a busy little bee while I was getting my beauty sleep."

She ignored his comment and continued, "The crime scene unit worked all night at Cole's house and basically came up with nothing. No fingerprints other than Cole's and Amberly's, and no evidence that anyone else had been in the house."

"That doesn't surprise me. Any chance of breakfast before we get started on this long day you have planned?"

She picked up a white paper bag that was between them on the console and tossed it into his lap. "Two bagels, one blueberry and one cinnamon raisin. I had a feeling you'd ask."

"Gee, I didn't know you cared." He opened up the bag to discover not only the two bagels, but also two small cups of cream cheese and a plastic knife.

"I don't," she replied. "But it appears that your creature comforts are very important to you."

"And your comforts aren't important to you?" he asked as he spread cream cheese over half of the cinnamon raisin bagel.

"Of course they are, but not so much when I'm working on a hot, active case."

"This is already at best a lukewarm case," he replied.

As she had yesterday, she wore a white blouse, a pair of dark slacks and sensible shoes. Her hair was a spill of strawberry silk across her shoulders and she smelled of fresh vanilla and sweet flowers.

She appeared not to be wearing a bit of makeup, but that did nothing to detract from Jackson's physical attraction to her. Chemistry… It was a whimsical animal that usually made a fool out of somebody.

He ate the bagel in four quick bites and wished for another cup of coffee to chase it down. But there was no way he intended to ask her to drive through the nearest coffee shop. He wasn't about to push his luck.

"Last night was more about my survival than creature comforts," he said soberly. "I'd been working nonstop on the case in Louisiana. Yesterday I'd had a plane ride from hell, no food to speak of all day and not enough brain power left to be adequate at my job. This could either be a sprint or a marathon, and I'm betting on a marathon, and so I needed last night to prepare myself for the long haul. Not that I owe you any explanations of my working habits or methods."

He settled back in his seat and stared out the passenger window. "Now, tell me about this John Merriweather," he said, deciding he was far better to focus on solving this crime than imagine what his partner might look like without her clothes.

MARJORIE STOOD JUST INSIDE Amberly's living room, a homey space decorated with pottery and bright colors and woven rugs celebrating her Native American heritage.

The room smelled of sage and sunshine, and it was obvious that a little boy resided here. The bookcases held not only pottery, but also puzzles and children's books about horses and dinosaurs. A large plastic dump truck sat next to the coffee table, the bed filled with tiny army men.

Jackson prowled the room like a well-educated burglar, with booties and gloves to leave no evidence that he'd ever been here. As he moved, she tried not to think about that moment when she'd walked into his motel room and he'd leaned out of the bathroom with just the thin white towel hanging low on his slim hips.

His bare chest, sleekly muscled and bronzed, had been more than magnificent. As she'd gotten that glimpse of it, for a long moment she'd forgotten how to breathe, and she hadn't been able to get the unwanted image out of her head.

He stopped and stared at the large painting above the fireplace. It depicted Amberly as an Indian princess on horseback. Her long dark hair emphasized doe eyes and high cheekbones. She was wild beauty captured on canvas.

Jackson turned to look at Marjorie at the same time she self-consciously shoved a strand of her hair behind an ear. "She's quite beautiful," he said, and then added, with a twinkle in his eyes, "But I much prefer blondes with just a hint of strawberry in their hair."

"Does it just come naturally to you? Kind of like breathing?" she asked sarcastically.

"Yeah, just like breathing," he replied with a genuine grin that warmed her despite her aggravation with him. He turned back to the painting. "Painted by her ex-husband?"

"Yes, John painted it." She'd already told him that John Merriweather was a famous painter who was known for Western settings and beautiful Native American portraits. Most of the Native women he painted looked like his ex-wife. She'd read an article in some magazine where John had talked about how Amberly was his muse.

"How did John take their divorce?" Jackson turned back to look at her.

She shrugged. "According to the local gossip, initially he took it rather hard. But I think they had become more like friends than husband and wife. Amberly once mentioned to me that John's greatest passion was his painting."

Jackson frowned. "I love my work, but I save my passion for living, breathing people."

Women. She knew he meant women. Not that it mattered to her what Jackson Revannaugh's personal passion might be. "Are you married?" The question fell from her lips before it had even formed in her head.

"No, and have no intention of ever getting married. My problem is that I love all women, but I've never found one who I haven't tired of after a week or so."

"So, you are a player," she said, having already suspected as much.

His blue eyes held an open honesty she wasn't sure she could believe. "On the contrary, I only date women who know I'm looking for a passing good time and nothing more serious. I don't toy with hearts or emotions. And now, shall we get back to the case?" He lifted a dark eyebrow wryly.

Heat warmed Marjorie's cheeks in an unmistakable blush. Thankfully he didn't comment on it but rather moved from the living room into the kitchen.

He hadn't even asked her if she was married or if she had a boyfriend. He probably thought she was too much of a witch to hold a man's attention for more than a minute.

She was, and that was the way she wanted it. She had enough on her plate with her job and helping to pay for the fancy apartment where her mother lived and believed she was still a wealthy heiress.

She didn't have time for men. She'd had one brief relationship years ago and he'd turned out to be untrustworthy, as she'd come to believe most men were. She'd been through enough men with her mother, seen what they were capable of, especially the handsome ones full of charm. Nope, she had already decided she'd eventually get a cat, but there would never be a man in the small house where she lived.

Of course, that didn't mean she would never have sex again. Like Jackson, if she did she'd just have to make it clear to her partner that she was a one-night stand—not a forever—kind of woman.

She snapped her attention back to realize Jackson had left the kitchen. It was easy to follow the sound of his heavy footsteps down the hallway to the bedrooms.

Focus on the job, she reprimanded herself, irritated that Jackson had somehow managed to throw her off her normal game, and she'd been working with him less than two hours this morning.

It took them only minutes to check out the bedrooms and return to the living room. "There doesn't appear to be anything here to tie into whatever happened at Cole's house in Mystic Lake," he said. "I think it's time we go talk to John Merriweather."

"He lives less than two blocks away." She checked her watch. It was a quarter after nine. Max would have already left for school and John would be waiting for them.

Within minutes they pulled into the driveway of John Merriweather's neat ranch house. Although John was a respected artist whose work was both expensive and in constant demand, he had remained in the house where he and Amberly had lived as a married couple over five years ago.

"John and Amberly lived here together when they were married," she explained to Jackson. "When they divorced, Amberly bought her house close by so that Max could stay near his father."

"Do they have a court-ordered child custody agreement?" Jackson asked.

"Not that I know of. I think they just winged it and it worked for them."

"We'll see if it was really working out that well, especially when a new man entered the picture," Jackson replied as he got out of the car. "I'll do the interview with him," he said in a clipped tone she hadn't heard before.

She hurried after him, wondering when she'd lost control as lead investigator. She'd allow Jackson to have his moment now, but then she would remind him that this was her case, and he'd simply been invited in to help.

John answered on the first knock. He was a handsome man with dark brown hair and hazel eyes. At the moment he wore a pair of jeans, an old T-shirt and a simmering panic that shone bright from his eyes.

Jackson took care of the introductions, and John sighed in relief. "Have you found them?" he asked as he allowed them entry into the house.

"No, and that's why we're here. We'd like to ask you some questions." Although the Southern accent remained, there was nothing of the lazy charmer in Jackson's demeanor. His eyes were an ice-blue as they gazed at John.

"Ask me questions about what?" John sank down to the sofa as if unable to stay on his feet beneath the intensity of Jackson's gaze.

Jackson remained standing, as did Marjorie, her gaze darting around the room with professional interest. Nice furniture, although the space had a lived-in look with a newspaper spread across the top of the coffee table and several matchbox cars on a highway built of paper on the floor.

The walls were filled with Merriweather's artistic genius, framed canvases of paintings in bright colors, including several of Amberly.

"How did you feel when your ex-wife married Cole Caldwell?" Jackson asked.

"I was happy for her…happy for them. All I ever wanted for Amberly was her happiness. What's this all about? Surely you can't think I had anything to do with whatever has happened to them." John's voice held a hint of outrage.

"Were you worried that your son might start to think of Cole as his daddy, cutting you out of his life?" Jackson's tone held an edge of suspicion that Marjorie instinctively knew he was doing on purpose.

"That's crazy," John scoffed. "My son loves me and I hope he and Cole love each other. A child can't have too many people to love them in their life."

"What did you do over the past weekend?" Jackson asked as he pulled his small notepad and pen from his shirt pocket.

John released an impatient sigh. "I had Max all weekend. Friday night we went to a movie, Saturday we went to the mall and did a little shopping and then ate at the food court, and then Sunday we hung out here all day." His hands clenched tight although he kept his voice calm. "You're wasting precious time here. I would never do anything to hurt Cole and Amberly, especially because they are important to my son. I would never do something like that to him."

He looked beseechingly at Marjorie. "Do you have children?"

She shook her head. "No, I don't." His question created a wistful ache inside her, one she quickly tamped down. In order to have any children she'd have to trust a man, and that wasn't in the cards for her.

"Then you can't understand the love a father has for his son." He half rose from the sofa. "You have to find them. Max needs his mother." Tears filled his eyes and he fell back against the cushions.

"Has Amberly mentioned any problems she's had with anyone lately?" Jackson pressed on.

John frowned. "No, not that I can think of. She went through a terrible trauma last year, but the person who tried to kill her was shot dead. Since then she's just seemed happy with Cole and hasn't mentioned any problems or issues with anyone."

Jackson wrote something down on his pad and then looked back at John. "How was your relationship with Cole?"

"Fine. It was fine." John's control appeared to be slipping. Marjorie saw his hands once again tighten into fists in his lap, and his voice had an edge that had been absent before. "Cole is a good man, and if I'd handpicked the man I wanted in Amberly's life, in my son's life, it would have been a man like him."

He looked at Marjorie again. "Please, find them. Max needs his mother. He doesn't know that they're missing. I just told him his mother was late in coming back from Mystic Lake. For God's sake, don't make me tell him she's missing again." The humble plea in John's voice shot straight to Marjorie's heart.

"Are you seeing anyone now?" Jackson asked, obviously unmoved by John's emotion.

"Seeing anyone? You mean, like, dating?" John shook his head. "Not at the present time."

"Have you dated at all since your divorce from Amberly?"

John's eyes took on a hard edge of their own. "You think I'm so obsessed with my ex-wife and that I killed her and her new husband?" he scoffed. "I've had several brief relationships since Amberly and I divorced."

"Why brief?" Jackson was relentless, and still with the cold demeanor that had Marjorie thanking her stars that he'd never be interrogating her.

"I have my work and I have Max—that doesn't leave me much time for romance." John stood. "Are we finished here? You're wasting valuable time when you could be out hunting who kidnapped Amberly and Cole."

"You think they've been kidnapped?" Jackson jotted something else in his notepad.

John raked a hand through his hair, his features once again twisted in agony. "I don't know. I don't know what in the hell happened to them. I just know that Amberly would never just disappear like this on Max unless something terrible happened. You've got to find them."

"We're going to," Marjorie said, cutting off anything else Jackson might want to say. She stepped toward where John stood and pulled one of her cards out of her pocket. "If you think of anything that might be helpful, if you remember anyone who might be a threat to Amberly or Cole, call me."

John took the card with shaking fingers and nodded. "And you'll let me know what's happening with the investigation?"

"We'll keep you up to date," Marjorie assured him.

"Like hell we will," Jackson said a few moments later when they were back in his car. "Right now John Merriweather is at the very top of my suspect list."

Marjorie shot him a look of surprise.

"Think about it, Maggie. Who has the most to gain from Amberly and Cole disappearing? Max's father, that's who. He has a great motive for wanting them gone."

She didn't want to even think about the fact that he'd just called her Maggie, something nobody else in her entire life had ever done. She didn't intend to reprimand him now, as right now she was considering what he'd said about John Merriweather.

"He might have a good motive to get rid of them in a sick sort of way, but he doesn't have opportunity. He had his son with him all weekend long," she replied.

She pulled out of the Merriweather driveway and headed in the direction of the Kansas City field office where they would next be interviewing Amberly's closest coworkers.

"I saw a picture of Max and his dad on the bookcase. What is he…about six?" Jackson asked.

"Seven," Marjorie replied. "I think he's going to be eight in a couple months."

"I don't know about you but when I was seven my father could have tucked me into bed and then left the house, gone to a movie, slept with a woman and been back home again before I woke up the next morning."

She slid him a curious glance. "And where would your mother have been while your father was out through the night hours?"

"Dead. She died when I was five, of cancer. But that really doesn't matter now—my point is that John could have easily slipped outside the house while Max slept, driven to Mystic Lake and done something to Amberly and Cole and been back before Max awoke the next morning."

"So, supposing he made that midnight run to Mystic Lake, then where are Amberly and Cole? If he killed them, why not just leave the bodies in the house?"

"Nobody said I had all the answers, darlin'. I just have theories."

"I think this one is kind of lame," she replied.

"Maybe," he agreed, the laid-back agent once again present. "John mentioned something about the last time a man tried to kill Amberly. What was that all about?"

"It's actually the case that brought Amberly and Cole together. Somebody was killing young women in Mystic Lake and leaving dream catchers hanging over their bodies. The mayor of Mystic Lake asked for FBI help, and since Director Forbes thought Amberly was the perfect agent to assist, because of the Native American overtones, she was sent to Mystic Lake to work with Cole."

She paused to make the turn into the parking area of the field office, a three-story brick building in the downtown area. "The perp eventually went after Amberly and trapped her in a rented storage unit. It was John's best friend and neighbor who had taken her."

She frowned in thought as she pulled into a parking place. "Ed...Ed Gershner was his name. He had some crazy notion that the only way John would be happy again was if Amberly was dead and John could finally forget her. Thankfully, Cole found Amberly, killed Ed and the rest, as they say, is history."

She turned off the engine and they both got out of the car. "Hopefully these interviews will go fairly quickly. It's got to be getting close to lunchtime by now," he said.

Marjorie hurried after his long strides, successfully stifling the impulse to knock him upside his head.

Chapter Three

Amberly Nightsong Caldwell's coworkers at the FBI field office had little to disclose about anyone who might want to harm her. She wasn't currently assigned to any active case. Her director knew she was in the middle of a transitional time in moving Cole into her home, and so he'd given her desk duty pushing paperwork, and regular hours until she and Cole got things settled.

Jackson had stepped back and allowed Marjorie to interview the players, since they were also her coworkers.

He quickly noticed that while the people they spoke to all appeared to respect Marjorie, none of them seemed to be particularly close to her. She was apparently a loner who didn't require friends.

Jackson had tons of men he counted as close friends in past partners and at the Baton Rouge field office. Jackson wasn't only considered a ladies' man—he was a man's man, as well.

He was the first one to invite a crew over to his place for drinks and chips and dip during a football game, or get together a group to do some horseback riding at nearby stables or head to a firing range for a little impromptu competition.

One thing had become increasingly clear to Jackson as the morning had gone on. Marjorie Clinton was one uptight woman. She smiled rarely and the few she sent his way were filled with either irritation or a strange curiosity, as if he were a species of animal she didn't know and certainly didn't trust.

She intrigued him. He was interested to know her background, what made her who she was today. It was unusual for him to care enough to want to know that much about a woman.

When they'd finally finished up with Amberly's coworkers, he'd insisted they find a place where they could sit and eat lunch before beginning the next phase of interviews in Mystic Lake.

"Don't look so miserable," he told her when they sat down across from each other in a booth in a nearby diner.

"We could have just done drive-through on the way to Mystic Lake and saved some time," she replied.

Jackson opened a menu and shoved it toward her. "Mystic Lake will still be there whether we take ten minutes doing drive-through or half an hour actually sitting and eating."

"Don't you feel any urgency?" she asked, leaning toward him, her green eyes shining brightly. Her lashes were long and dark brown and he noticed, not for the first time that day, that she smelled of the fresh scent of a fabric softener combined with a hint of wildflowers.

"Ladybug, we're past the point of urgency. Urgency should have happened Saturday or Sunday. I wonder how the burgers are here?" He shouldn't be thinking about how good she smelled or the fact that he'd like to see a genuine smile from her directed at him.

"Who cares? I have a case of two missing people, and a partner who only wants to know when his next meal is due."

"Do you have many friends?" he asked.

She blinked twice and sat back. He knew she'd worked up a head of steam about taking the time out for lunch and probably was ticked off by the use of a pet name. His question had caught her off guard.

Her cheeks dusted a beautiful pink. "Actually, no. I don't have a lot of friends. I work all the overtime I can get and I spend my free time either sleeping or visiting with my mother."

"And your father?"

She opened her menu and lowered her gaze. "He died when I was ten."

"I'm sorry. It must have been tough for you and your mother."

"We got by," she replied, and still didn't meet his gaze.

"You're more comfortable if we talk about the case?"

He was rewarded with a flash of her eyes as she gazed up at him intently. "Yes," she said. "Unfortunately I don't think this is tied to anything Amberly was currently working on. Nobody we spoke to indicated she was having problems with anyone."

They were interrupted by the arrival of a blonde waitress with large breasts and a name tag that read June. "Hey, sweet June bug, how about you get us a couple of burgers and fries," he said.

"And what would you like to drink?" She practically tittered the words as she blushed at Jackson.

"I'll take a diet cola," Marjorie said stiffly.

"And I'll take a regular," Jackson replied.

As the waitress left the table with a swing of her hips, Marjorie shot him a wicked stare. "You just can't help yourself, can you?"

"Maybe I don't want to help myself," he replied, and leaned forward. "Do you know how many jackasses June bug probably puts up with on a daily basis? Bad tippers, chronic complainers... What's wrong with giving her a little ray of sunshine. It cost me nothing and made her smile."

She studied him for a long moment. "I'm not sure if I like you or not, Special Agent Revannaugh."

He grinned. "Don't worry. You've really only known me for less than a day. I'll grow on you."

"Right, like moss," she said dryly.

"Okay, just to get on your good side, we'll talk about the case. You're right. I think if we're going to find answers they are going to be in Mystic Lake. There has been no ransom demand, so if they were kidnapped it wasn't for money."

"They were kidnapped," she said with a certainty. "That's the only thing that could keep Amberly away from her son." She frowned thoughtfully. "We don't even know for sure who the intended victim was. One was probably the victim and the other was collateral damage."

"If Amberly was the intended victim, then we already have a suspect with a motive in John," he replied. "We'll see what we turn up in Mystic Lake and see if

Cole might have been working on a case that caused somebody to want revenge of some kind."

"I still can't believe that John would do anything to hurt Cole or Amberly," she replied.

"Yeah, but one of her coworkers mentioned that after Ed the potential killer was killed, John tried one last time to get back with his ex-wife," Jackson reminded her.

"But it obviously went nowhere and Amberly and John remained friends. Cole and Amberly got married and everyone moved on with their lives."

"At least on the surface," he replied.

The waitress returned with their drinks, flashing Jackson a wink as she placed his before him. "Burgers will be right up," she said.

"Thanks, June bug," he replied.

"Do you suffer from multiple personality disorder?" Marjorie asked.

Jackson nearly snorted pop through his nose. "What's that supposed to mean?"

"When you were interviewing John earlier you were sharp, no-nonsense and on top of your professional game, but now you're totally different. You're a laid-back flirting machine."

"Flirting machine. Hmm, I like that," he said in amusement and then sobered. "Maggie, if you play this game too long without being able to compartmentalize, you burn out quickly," he replied. "If I were to make a prediction, I'd guess that you're going to burn out fast if you approach all of your cases with the same intensity you're already using to attack this one."

At that moment June arrived with their burgers, and for a few minutes they both focused on their food.

Marjorie ate quickly, obviously eager to get back on the road and moving.

"So, who are we talking to in Mystic Lake?" he asked as he dragged a French fry through a pool of ketchup.

"Our point person there is Deputy Roger Black. He wasn't at the scene last night but we're to meet him in his office when we hit town. He's acting sheriff until Cole is found," she said.

"Has he managed to get us any suspects? Mentioned anything Cole was working on?"

"I've only had a brief conversation with him and we didn't get into the details. I'm hoping he'll have some information when we meet with him." She looked at her watch and then quickly took another bite of her burger.

"How long have you been on the job?" he asked.

"Two years. I joined the FBI when I turned thirty. I was a cop before that." She used a napkin to dab her mouth. "What about you?"

"Seven years. I was twenty-eight when they tapped me for recruitment. And like you, before that I was working as a homicide cop and working with a behavioral unit to aid in profiling violent offenders. My work there caught the FBI's eyes and here I am."

"But there's no indication that what we're dealing with here is a particularly violent offender." Her eyes shimmered with the need to believe that.

Jackson sighed. He'd made a vow long ago to himself that he would never, ever lie to a woman, no matter how painful the truth might be.

"It's too early to know," he finally replied. "All we

know for sure right now is that it appears that nothing violent occurred at Cole's house."

A look of pain tightened her features. She might appear uptight and in control, but Jackson had a feeling she was soft, too soft for the job she was doing.

"I'm hoping at least Deputy Black can give us somewhere to begin," Marjorie said when they were once again in the car and headed to Mystic Lake.

"Have you considered the possibility that they might be dead?" Jackson asked softly.

He saw the impact of his words in the swift etch of pain that once again crossed her features, in the tightening of her fingers around the steering wheel. "It's too early in the investigation to come to that conclusion. We have a lot of things to accomplish before we even consider that."

"It's been four days since anyone has heard from them." He wanted to prepare her for whatever they might discover. He was also surprised to realize that he somehow wanted to protect her.

He chalked it up to the fact that she was a relatively new agent while he was a seasoned veteran who had seen the horrible things people were capable of doing to each other.

"I know, but we have absolutely no evidence to support that they've been murdered."

"Right now we don't even have the evidence to support that they've been kidnapped," he reminded her.

"All I know for sure is that something bad has happened to them and we need to figure out what it was, who it is who's kept Amberly away from her son."

Jackson didn't want to remind her that the case he'd been working on in Bachelor Moon had involved three people who had gone missing and had yet to be found. No answers, no closure...nothing.

Still, he couldn't imagine how this case in Mystic Lake, Missouri, would be related to the case in Bachelor Moon, Louisiana. The two small towns were about a thousand miles away from each other. It had to be some sort of strange coincidence.

He hoped it was just a coincidence, because if the two cases were tied together he knew with certainty that they were way over their head.

"I'VE GOT A COUPLE OF NAMES of people for you to check out, although I don't have any evidence that either of them were involved." Roger Black looked ill at ease seated in the chair behind the large oak desk that belonged to his boss.

"What I'm hoping is that Cole decided to surprise Amberly with an impromptu late honeymoon and they're off on some exotic island enjoying their time alone," he added.

"Did Cole mention a trip?" Marjorie asked, hoping that there might be a possibility of a happy ending, after all. Maybe John had forgotten plans for a honeymoon that the couple had.

"Nothing specific, but it wasn't too long ago he said he had a mind to surprise Amberly with a trip to the Bahamas," Roger replied.

"Have you checked financials? Talked to airlines?" Jackson asked.

Roger swept a hand through his brown hair. "To be honest with you, we haven't done much of anything since we heard the Feds were being called in. According to the mayor, you are in charge. I've got my men ready to cooperate and do whatever you tell us to do."

"We've already lost a lot of time," Marjorie said.

Roger shrugged. "We didn't really get worried about them until last night. It's not a crime for two consenting adults to take off somewhere or not be where they are supposed to be."

"The first thing we want you to do is assign somebody to look at both Cole and Amberly's financials, see if anything has moved since last Friday night," Jackson said. "Check back over the last three months or so. If Cole bought tickets to an exotic island, then we'll find proof of that."

Roger nodded. "I'll get Deputy Ray McCloud on it right away. He's our techie freak. If there's a paper trail, so to speak, of anything like that, he'll find it."

"I also want you to assign a couple of officers to walk the streets, ask questions and see if we can find anyone who had any contact with the missing couple after Friday night. And you mentioned a couple of names for us?" Marjorie asked.

She wanted action. She needed to be doing something to move the investigation forward as quickly as possible. Jackson was right—she worked like a dog until conclusions were reached and bad guys were arrested. She was a hare, not a tortoise.

"I know Cole was having some issues with Natalie Redwing," Roger said.

Jackson pulled out his notepad and pen. "What kind of problems?"

"She was kind of, like, stalking him." Roger gave a dry laugh. "Cole thought she was harmless, but irritating." He gave them her address.

"Who else?" Marjorie asked.

"Jeff Maynard. He's a bartender at Bledsoe's on Main Street. He didn't like Cole and he definitely didn't like Amberly. He's a hothead loser, although I doubt he has the brains to kidnap a couple of people and not leave any clues behind. Off the top of my head those are the only two I've ever heard about Cole having any issues with."

Minutes later, armed with address information, Jackson and Marjorie left the small sheriff's office and headed out to interview both new suspects.

"You can do the interviewing with Jeff Maynard and I'll take Natalie Redwing," Jackson said.

"Why doesn't it surprise me that you'd want to talk to the woman and assign me the hothead loser?" Marjorie said dryly.

Jackson gave her that slow, lazy slide of his lips into a smile that heated places inside her that had never been warm before. "I'm hoping you can find a little charm and twist that hothead loser right around your little finger."

"Yeah, right, I've been holding out on you with the charm thing," Marjorie replied sarcastically.

She was aware of Jackson's gaze lingering on her as she focused on Main Street and searched for Bledsoe's tavern. It was late enough in the afternoon that Jeff Maynard should be working.

"I think you might be hiding a little bit of charm under a basket and I've decided it's my goal in life to figure out how to get that basket off your head."

Marjorie couldn't help herself—laughter bubbled to her lips and she shook her head. "You're a funny man, Agent Revannaugh." She pulled into a parking place in front of Bledsoe's, a long, low building at the edge of town.

"You know, that's the first time I've seen a genuine smile on your lips or heard laughter from you. You should do it more often. It definitely becomes you."

"I'm not a laughing kind of woman," she replied as she turned off the car engine. "I haven't had much to laugh about in my life."

"Then my second job is to change that," he replied.

"Duty calls." She got out of the car and slammed the door, more touched by Jackson's words than she wanted to admit. She couldn't let him get to her. She'd seen what men like him had done to her mother's life, to her life, and she was not going to be one of those women who fell for the charm and never saw the callous calculation beneath.

At just after four in the afternoon, Bledsoe's already had a few customers seated on stools at the long bar. It was semidark inside and reeked of booze and a faint underlying hint of urine.

It was the kind of place where the clientele was tough, bar fights occurred on a regular basis and nobody came for a social event. A jukebox played an old country song about a broken heart and a Texas man, but Marjorie was beginning to think it wasn't the tall, handsome cowboys you had to watch out for, it was the smooth-talking Southerners.

As she approached the bar, she pulled out her official identification from her purse, careful to keep the side of her purse that had a built-in gun holster against her body. She went toward the dark-haired bartender, feeling no need to show any more authority than her badge, but she was prepared, should that change.

"Smells like Feds to me," the bartender said as he slowly wiped a glass dry.

"Ah, nice to know you have a good sense of smell," Marjorie said, forcing a pleasant smile to her lips. She almost felt as if she had something to prove to her partner, that she could be as charming as she needed to be while talking to a potential suspect.

"You're cuter than your partner." He set down the glass and jabbed a finger in the direction of Jackson, who stood a couple of inches behind her.

"Thanks. I'm smarter, too. But I let him think he's smarter because he has a huge ego."

Jackson cleared his voice as the bartender barked a dry laugh.

"We're looking for Jeff Maynard," she said.

"You found him, sweetheart, but as far as I know I haven't done anything to get special attention from the FBI." His eyes were dark with more than a hint of wariness.

"What do you know about Cole and Amberly Caldwell's disappearance?" Marjorie asked.

"Only that I'm not gonna cry in my beer tonight over it." He picked up a wet cloth and gave the bar a desultory swipe. "Look, I know you're here because everyone in Mystic Lake knows I don't like Cole. I have a problem with authority figures," he added with a smirk.

Marjorie leaned closer to the bar, closer to the man she knew might possibly have had something to do with Cole and Amberly's disappearance. "All authority?" she asked with a teasing lilt to her voice.

She sensed Jackson leaning closer behind her, but she kept her gaze focused on Jeff, as if he were the most important person on the face of the earth. A small, lewd grin curved his lips. "Well, maybe not all. I wouldn't mind getting over it by maybe hand-cuffing you to my bed."

Marjorie blinked in shock and leaned backward, bumping into Jackson's firmly muscled chest. "I must protest," Jackson said in his pleasant Southern drawl. "If anyone is going to handcuff this little lady to his bed, it's going to be me."

Marjorie felt as if she were having an out of body experience. "Where were you this past weekend?" she asked Jeff, trying to get her feet beneath her and get the conversation back on track.

The smirk disappeared from Jeff's face. "Friday is my night off. I was out with buddies. Saturday night I worked my usual shift here, from four until close."

"And where did you go with these buddies on Friday night?" Marjorie asked. She didn't bother to pull out her pen and pad. She knew instinctively that Jackson already had his out.

"We were at Jimmy Tanner's place, playing poker. He's newly divorced, thanks to Cole and Amberly and their prying into private lives when they were investigating the murders of those women last year."

"Jimmy Tanner, what's his address?" Marjorie asked, realizing she'd just added another name to a potential suspect with a motive of revenge.

"At the moment he's living at the Mystic Lake Motel on the south side of town," Jeff replied. "His wife really took him to the cleaners in the divorce."

By the time they left Bledsoe's, they had not only added Jimmy Tanner's name to their list, but also Raymond Chandler, who had also been at the supposed poker party on Friday night.

"I'm impressed, Ms. Maggie. I think there's a bit of naughty woman trapped inside you," Jackson said once they were back in the car.

"Don't be ridiculous," she scoffed, cheeks far too warm. "There's no naughty inside of me. I'm by the book, rigid and uptight. Trust me, Jackson, I know who I am."

"I wonder," he mused. She kept her mouth firmly closed, not wanting to know what he wondered. "Let's head on back to Kansas City," he said. "We can drive back out here and start with this Natalie Redwing first thing in the morning."

"Why not do it now?" Marjorie asked.

Jackson looked at his watch. "It's going to be close to six by the time we make it back to Kansas City. I say we order a pizza and sit down and go through what we know, figure out who needs to be interviewed next and get a general idea of where we are."

"Right now it feels like we're nowhere," she replied.

"Exactly. It might surprise you to know that I can be a by-the-book kind of guy despite my huge ego."

She glanced over to catch him smiling that sexy grin of his. "So, what does that mean?"

"It means I'd like to feed my notes into my laptop and see if we really have nothing or if we've already made any connections that might lead somewhere. I also want to utilize some resources I have with the agency to double-check bank records, travel and anything else that might pop up with Amberly or Cole's names."

"But you just assigned that task for Deputy Black to take care of," she replied.

"You know our resources are better than theirs."

"Okay, sounds like a plan," she replied somewhat reluctantly. She had a feeling being in a motel room with Jackson Revannaugh for any reason probably wasn't the best idea.

Chapter Four

He couldn't get the vision of her smile, the sound of her laughter, out of his head. Something about Marjorie Clinton was getting under his skin, Jackson thought as he paid the pizza delivery boy an hour later.

He carried the box to the table and chairs that sat in front of the windows in the motel room. His laptop was open to a file labeled Mystic Lake/Kansas City.

While they had awaited the food delivery, the two of them had sat side by side as he fed into the file the bits and pieces of information they had attained so far in the case.

He'd tried not to notice how shiny her hair was beneath the lamp that hung from the ceiling over the center of the table. He'd tried not to draw in the sweet scent of her that made him think of tangled sheets and slick bodies.

The pizza was a compromise. His half was spicy pepperoni and sausage, and hers was mushroom and green pepper. It was just an indication to him that they were complete opposites and he had no business thinking about what she would look like naked, how her lips would taste or if he could evoke any passion that might be hidden beneath her emotional walls.

Surely these thoughts were only because they were in a relatively intimate setting and there was no question that he was physically attracted to her.

She looked relaxed for the first time since they'd met. Her blouse was unbuttoned at the top, revealing her delicate collarbone, and her body appeared to hold none of the tension of the day.

"So, tomorrow we check out the names we have of people from Mystic Lake," she said as he opened the box and handed her several napkins. She leaned closer to him to look at his computer screen. "Jimmy Tanner, Raymond Chandler and Natalie Redwing—we should be able to have those interviews finished by noon, and maybe one of them will give us more information."

"We also need to check back in with Deputy Black and maybe interview some of the other deputies who worked with Cole." He waited until she took a piece of the pie and then he grabbed a piece for himself. "It's possible that somebody who worked for Cole didn't have his back."

Marjorie frowned thoughtfully. "We might reinterview John Merriweather again to see if he's thought of anything new."

"He's still at the top of my suspect list," Jackson replied and then bit into the slice he had folded in half.

"I'm anxious to talk to Jimmy Tanner and Raymond Chandler to see how well they can corroborate Jeff's poker game alibi for Friday night," she replied.

"He seems so obvious as a suspect," Jackson replied, sorry when she leaned back in her chair and put some distance between them. "He didn't make any bones about the fact that he doesn't like the sheriff."

"Sometimes it's the most obvious suspect that turns

out to be the perp." She wiped her mouth with the napkin and for the next few minutes they fell into silence as they devoured the pizza.

He liked watching her. She had the kind of expressive face that let him know when her thoughts were happy or somber. He found himself wishing he knew what was going through her mind.

He chided himself irritably. Marjorie wasn't a player. She was with him now because she was assigned to work this case with him, and when the case was over she'd probably never think of him again.

And that was the way it was supposed to be, he reminded himself. He glanced up to find her impossibly green eyes locked with his. "You've gotten very quiet," she said. "What are you thinking about?"

"I'm wondering why you don't have some boyfriend ticked off because you're working with an irresistible, handsome devil like me."

She tossed the last of a piece of crust into the box and wiped her mouth once again. "I don't have a boyfriend because I don't want a boyfriend. I'm perfectly comfortable alone." She hesitated a moment and her eyes deepened in hue. "I had enough scheming stepfathers in my life to be done with the idea of relationships or marriage for the rest of my life."

"What do you mean by scheming stepfathers?"

She hesitated, as if weighing how much of herself she was willing to give to him. "When my father died, he left my mother a very wealthy woman, wealthy enough and lonely enough that she was easy pickings for smooth-talking con men to take advantage of."

She worried her napkin in her lap as Jackson's pizza suddenly sat heavily in his stomach. "It took three husbands to swindle her out of her last dime and leave her broke and alone." She shrugged. "I'm not much inclined to share anything with anyone after that experience."

"I'm sorry," Jackson said, knowing it was inadequate and also recognizing that if she ever found out about his own father, she'd hate Jackson and would never believe that he wasn't a chip off the old block.

"It's not your fault, and I have Mom settled in a nice apartment, surrounded by beautiful furnishings so she can feel like she's still living a bit of the good life."

"And what has that done for your lifestyle?" he asked.

Once again she shrugged. "I don't require much. I've managed to get myself a little two-bedroom house that's just right for me."

Although she didn't say it, although she didn't even intimate it, Jackson knew she must be making personal sacrifices to keep her mother happy. An unexpected pain ripped through his heart, along with a lot of guilt he knew he didn't deserve but hadn't been able to shake from his psyche for years.

"You know you shouldn't judge all men by what happened to your mother," he said.

"I don't. I'm a cautious woman, Jackson. I just don't take chances, not in my job as an FBI agent and not in my personal life."

"Being too cautious can close you off from important experiences," he replied.

"I recognize that and I'm okay with it. My life is just the way I like it—predictable and without chaos."

"And love equals chaos to you?" He raised a dark eyebrow.

"Not necessarily." She gave a small, dry laugh.

"What are you doing? Trying to be my life coach? You, who has never met a woman he didn't like, who probably changes girlfriends as often as you change your shirt? You've already told me you aren't the marrying kind, so why is it any different for me not to be the marrying kind?"

He knew it was crazy, but what he wanted to tell her was that she deserved a man who would cherish her, a man who could bring that magical and elusive laughter to her easily and often.

"You're right. I shouldn't give relationship advice to anyone," he finally said.

"So, what are your personal issues when it comes to marriage and long-term commitments?"

Her question surprised him, and he didn't have an answer that he was willing to share with her. "I just don't think I'd do it very well," he replied. He gave her an irreverent smile. "You know, so many women, so little time," he said flippantly.

Her emerald eyes narrowed as her gaze held his. "I wonder what baggage you're carrying around."

He leaned back in his chair with surprise. "What makes you think I have baggage?"

"Maybe it's like sensing like," she replied. "I know what my baggage is and I think I'm not the only one seated at this table who might have some issues."

He could easily fall into the depths of her eyes—*so green*—and he felt as if her gaze was so intense she was looking inside his soul, seeking answers he had sworn he would never give to any woman.

She finally broke the gaze and glanced toward the window, where the sheer curtains couldn't cover the darkness of night that had fallen while they'd talked.

"It's getting late and we need to get an early start in the morning. We have a lot to accomplish tomorrow. It's time for me to head home."

"You're right," he agreed, wondering how the conversation had gotten so personal so quickly. He'd have to be more careful—she was far too easy to talk to, and there were far too many secrets and shames in his life to let down his guard.

They both got up from the table, and the windows in front of them exploded inward. Instinctively Jackson grabbed Marjorie and pulled her to the floor.

He rolled her to the opposite side of the room, where they would be partially shielded by the edge of the bed as the tat-tat-tat of an automatic weapon resounded and bullets shredded the curtains, slammed into the walls, and furniture splintered.

He lay on top of her while the world around them exploded, and knew that there was nothing more he could do but wait and pray that when the shooting stopped they would both still be alive.

PICTURE FRAMES SMASHED and fell from the walls, and Marjorie braced herself for a piercing bullet to find her, even though Jackson's body covered hers.

She could feel his heartbeat, as rapid, as frantic as her own, and the shooting seemed to last forever. A squeal of tires was audible from the broken windows, and after that, utter silence.

For several long moments they remained in place, hearts racing against each other's, the slight scent of pepperoni coming from him. He finally rose slightly and asked, "Are you all right?"

"I…I don't know," she admitted truthfully. "I'm not shot, but I'm a little dazed."

Siren screams filled the night, drawing closer, and the scent of cordite was thick in the air. "I wondered what it might be like for me to be on top of you on a floor or in my bed, but this wasn't exactly what I had in mind," he said.

She shoved him off her and he stood. "Do you always have sex on the brain?" she asked as she got to her feet. "Don't you realize that somebody just tried to kill us?"

Cherry swirls just outside the motel room indicated that the police had arrived. Jackson grinned at her. "Snapped you right out of that daze, didn't I?"

He was right. The fogginess in her brain was gone and she was acutely aware of everything. "It was probably some heartbroken woman who followed you here from Baton Rouge to put a bullet through your black heart."

"Or could be a man you cut off at the knees with your attitude and sharp tongue," he replied.

At that moment several officers raced into the room, guns drawn and terse expressions on their faces. "You both okay?"

"No," Marjorie replied. "He's an egotistical ass."

"And she's an uptight witch," Jackson said. "But other than that, we're both fine. Unfortunately the room appears to be a bit of a mess."

Marjorie looked around and her knees threatened to buckle. "A bit of a mess" was definitely an understatement. The walls were riddled with bullet holes, glass was everywhere and even the bed hadn't escaped the carnage, as tufts of mattress padding peeked out of gaping holes. It was a wonder—no, it was a miracle—that they had survived unscathed.

She sank down on the edge of the bed, unable to take in how near death she had come. She listened as Jackson made introductions to the officer who appeared in charge and then told him what had happened.

"I have no idea what kind of vehicle the perp was in, but it was definitely an Uzi that was used to shoot up the place. I know the sound," Jackson said.

The officer wore a tag that identified him as Lieutenant Larry Segal. "Do you have any idea who might be behind this attack?"

"We're investigating a case of a couple of missing persons in Mystic Lake. Apparently there's somebody who doesn't like the questions we're asking people," Jackson replied.

"Apparently," Segal replied. He yelled to one of his other officers. "Let's get a crime scene unit in here. We need to find as many bullets as possible." He motioned for Jackson and Marjorie to follow him outside the room.

Marjorie grabbed her bag from the floor next to the table and clutched it to her chest, the feel of her gun in the purse holster somewhat comforting. Jackson's laptop computer was toast, exploded into pieces of plastic and metal.

As they stepped out into the darkness of the night, Marjorie's knees still felt wobbly and the sound of the bullets slamming into a variety of items echoed in her head.

"What's going on?" A short rotund man came running toward them. "What in the hell happened here?" He threw out his arms, his round face screwed up in anger. "Drug deal gone bad?" He glared at Jackson and then eyed Marjorie. "Are you a prostitute working out of my motel? Did you tick off some john or what?"

Marjorie nearly swallowed her tongue in shock. Never in a million years had anyone ever mistaken her for a hooker. Jackson took a step closer to her, as if to protect her from the angry little man. "This is FBI business," he said.

"I don't give a damn if it's YMCA business, what I want to know is who is going to pay for this damage? I run a respectable motel here."

"Wayne, don't worry, we'll figure it all out," Lieutenant Segal said.

"Somebody better figure it out fast. This is bad for business and I need somebody to get this room back in shape as soon as possible."

Marjorie imagined she could see fumes rising off Wayne's nearly bald head. "I'll call my director and he'll see that the repairs on the room are taken care of after the local officials are finished processing things." She was appalled to hear her voice tremble slightly.

She straightened her back and tried to mentally pull herself together. The last thing she wanted was for Jackson to believe she wasn't up to the job, that she couldn't handle danger when it reared its ugly head.

Wayne's strident voice grew more distant as one of the officers led him back toward the motel office. Jackson and Segal were still talking, and she was just trying to process what had just happened. Two patrol cars were parked in a way to deny entry to any other vehicle into the motel parking lot.

She'd never experienced anything like this before.

As long as she'd been working in the job, she'd never had her life personally threatened.

Death had whispered on the back of her neck, and even now a shiver tried to work up her spine. Surely it was normal to feel this way after such an experience.

"Are you okay?" A deep voice came from beside her, jolting her out of her thoughts.

She turned to see Officer Kevin Winslow standing next to her. He was a young cop and she was surprised to see that his brown eyes held the same kind of horror she felt.

"I'm fine, although it all feels kind of surreal at the moment."

He glanced toward the open motel room door with the shattered windows in the front. "I think I probably would have had a heart attack," he admitted.

They had just been sitting at the table in front of those windows, she thought. If they'd waited another moment to get up, there was no question in her head that both of them would have been killed.

Her gaze shifted to Jackson, who was still speaking with the lieutenant. "I have a good partner. He got me to the floor before either of us was shot."

Kevin nodded. "That's what good partners are for. We're just glad we're investigating a shooting and not a double homicide."

"Trust me, I'm glad about that, too."

Kevin drifted away as Jackson walked toward Marjorie. He held a duffel bag and clothes on hangers. They were surrounded by chaos, swirling lights and the sound of radios, and still he smiled as his gaze locked with hers. "Well, Maggie, darlin', you sure know how to show a man an exciting time," he said when he was close enough for her to hear him above the din.

"That was a bit too exciting for my blood," she replied honestly. "So what happens now?"

"The local authorities are taking it from here, and it looks like I need a place to stay. Didn't you mention you had a nice little two-bedroom house?" Even in the semidarkness that surrounded him, she saw the upward quirk of his eyebrow. The expression only enhanced his attractiveness, by giving him a slightly rakish appearance.

The last thing she wanted was this man under her roof, but it was late and it would take hours to go through proper channels to get him into another motel room.

Besides, it would be churlish of her to turn him away after what they'd just been through. He'd basically saved her life. Surely she could give him a bed for a night. Certainly, he would make other arrangements in the morning.

"I'll warn you, the bedroom is quite small," she finally said.

"Does it have a bed?" he asked. She nodded. "Then it sounds perfect to me."

"Then let's go," she replied.

Amazingly all of the bullets that had flown had been specifically targeted at the motel window. Her car parked in front had no damage, which made her think that the shooter or shooters had been proficient with their automatic weapons.

The minute Jackson slid into the passenger seat, she caught a whiff of his cologne, and her brain exploded with the tactile memory of lying beneath him.

His body had been hard and had seemed to completely surround her in a cocoon of safety, of warmth, that she'd never felt before in her life. Despite the situation, there had been something erotic about his weight on top of her as their hearts beat a frantic rhythm.

"We're going to have to figure out how in the hell this happened," he said once they were in her car and headed to her house. "Who knew where I was staying?"

"Me, of course, and my director and probably a few other people at headquarters." She tried to focus on the conversation and not the thoughts of how she'd felt beneath him. *Be a professional,* she told herself. Obviously Jackson was in agent mode, as she should be, as well.

"The only people we spoke to about this case were agents who had worked with Amberly in the past and they all said she was having no personal issues with anyone. I find it hard to believe that somebody inside headquarters was responsible for what just happened."

"Maybe, maybe not. The only other possibility is that we shook up somebody's cage in Mystic Lake today and we made them damned uncomfortable. If that's the case then we were followed when we left there to head to the motel."

Stricken, Marjorie cast him a quick glance. "I didn't even think about the possibility of anyone following us from there to here. I didn't pay attention to the cars behind us." She squeezed her fingers around the steering wheel, mentally beating herself up for being so careless.

"Don't worry your pretty head," he replied easily. "I didn't think about it, either. But we have now been warned, and we have to proceed from here with caution. We're poking somebody and they don't like it."

Proceed with caution. The words whirled around in her head. Somehow she felt as if she was already abandoning that idea by inviting him into her home.

Chapter Five

She'd told him her home was small, but when she pulled into the driveway of the cracker box–sized place, Jackson was a bit shocked.

He was by no means a snob, but the size of the house reminded him of his earlier thought that she was making sacrifices to keep her mother happy. The entire house would fit into the living room of his apartment.

As they walked through the front door and she flipped on a light in the living room, the aura of sacrifice continued. The room was furnished with a cheap futon, two end tables and a bookcase that looked as if it had been thrown out on somebody's lawn for trash pickup. A small television sat on the top shelf, and he would bet his next month's salary that she didn't even have basic cable.

"It isn't much, but it's home," she said, as if seeing the room through his eyes.

"It's just fine," he assured her. "If you could just show me to my bedroom I'll stow my things away and then we'll talk and see what our next move should be."

"Follow me," she said. She led him down a hall-way that was little more than a few steps and stopped at the first doorway. "This is the guest room, and the bathroom is across the hall."

Jackson stepped into the room, which was just big enough to hold a double bed, a single nightstand and a chest of drawers. The room was painted a light shade of blue and the spread was a geometric design of light and dark blue. Nothing fancy, just functional. He would have expected nothing more from her.

"This is perfect," he said as he tossed his duffel bag on the bed. "Do you have a computer and internet connection here?"

"I do. I have an area in the kitchen where I keep my laptop. You're welcome to use it until you get something to replace your own."

"I'm not doing anything tonight, although I think maybe a cup of coffee might be in order. I don't know about you, but I've got adrenaline firing through me, and there's no way I can go to sleep right now."

"Why don't you get settled in and I'll go make half a pot of coffee," she replied. She got halfway out of the doorway and then turned back to look at him, her eyes simmering with emotion. "Jackson, thank you again for saving my life tonight. When those bullets slammed through the window I couldn't even process what had happened. If you hadn't grabbed me…" Her voice trailed off.

He smiled at her. "Darlin', it was my pleasure."

Her cheeks dusted with color and she quickly disappeared from his sight. He turned to his duffel bag and unzipped it to begin to unpack.

As he stowed underwear, jeans and T-shirts into the drawers, his mind whirled. Somebody had tried to kill them. Faces of the people they'd interacted with since his arrival in town flew through his head. Had they already made contact with the person or persons responsible for Cole and Amberly's disappearance, or had small-town gossip let the perp know they were in town and asking questions?

He'd flung Marjorie down and covered her to save her life, and yet as the bullets had flown all around them he'd been far too conscious of the press of her full breasts against his chest, of the sweet scent of her that made him want to press his lips into the hollow of her throat.

He hung the clothes he'd managed to get from the motel closet in the much smaller closet in the bedroom. He then grabbed the small leather bag that contained his toiletries and carried it into the bathroom.

Staring at his reflection for a moment, he forced himself to change the track of his brain. He couldn't think about Marjorie as a desirable woman now—he had to think like an FBI agent who had just nearly been killed.

The scent of freshly brewed coffee drew him down the short hallway and into a kitchen that had a small table for two, a short counter and a built-in desk that was obviously her workstation. A laptop was on top along with an all-in-one printer/fax machine and phone. She'd probably spent more money on her work equipment than in the entire furnishings of the house.

She turned from the counter as he entered the room. "Coffee is ready," she said.

Her lips pressed tight and her shoulders were tense. Her face was unusually pale. Her blouse had dirt streaks, and a button was missing, and her hair was a riotous mess of shiny red-gold strands.

She looked like a woman who had been to hell and hadn't yet fully realized that she'd really made her way back.

He walked over to where she stood and placed his hands gently on her slender shoulders. "Sit. I'll get the coffee." She opened her mouth to protest, but he quickly slid his finger over her lips. "Trust me, I got this."

She nodded and walked over to the table where she crumpled into the chair as if the weight of the world was on her shoulders.

Jackson turned to face the counter and opened the cabinet door above the coffeemaker, unsurprised to find the three cups nestled side by side. "Cream or sugar?" he asked as he poured the brew.

"Black is fine."

When he turned back with the cups in hand, she was once again sitting upright, the paleness gone and her eyes glittering with a hint of anger. Good, he needed her angry and hopefully not at him. Anger channeled in the right direction would make them both driven to find answers.

He set one cup before her, then took the seat across from her and wrapped his hands around the warmth of his cup. "Tomorrow I want you to get the names of every single person here in Kansas City who knew the motel where I'd been set to stay. First thing in the morning, we're going to check out John Merriweather's alibi for tonight. He's the only person we interviewed here in the city."

She nodded, her eyes gleaming with a steely strength he found ridiculously hot. "And then we head back to Mystic Lake and continue our interviews there, along with checking any alibis of people we interacted with there today."

She took a sip of her coffee and her gaze remained locked with his. "Was this like what was happening in Bachelor Moon and the case you were pulled off?" She set her cup back on the table.

"Nothing like what happened tonight. None of the people working that case came under any kind of a threat. Tonight wasn't just a scare tactic, it was attempted murder."

Her eyes paled a bit. "I know and I darn straight want to find out who was behind that gun."

Jackson grimaced with frustration. "I wish I would have been able to get a glimpse of the car."

She smiled at him and for a moment he wanted to get lost in it, in her. "You couldn't cover the window and me at the same time. I'm grateful you made the decision you did." Her smile faded. "I just wish we knew if we've shaken up somebody here in Kansas City or somebody in Mystic Lake. It would be easier to investigate if we only had one place to look."

"Shame on Amberly and Cole for living in two places and making this more difficult on us," he said wryly. He broke their gaze, glancing around the room in an effort to stay focused on the case and not how much her smile had warmed him or how soft her lips had been beneath his fingers.

He noticed a red light blinking on her telephone answering machine. "It looks like you have some phone messages. Maybe you should check them out, make sure one of the calls isn't from our motel visitors. It would be a boon if our perp was the chatty type."

She took another sip of her coffee and then got

up from the table and approached the answering machine. The first message was an offer for a free estimate from a siding company. She erased it and then a female voice filled the room.

"Marjorie, when are you going to come visit me? It feels like it's been weeks. Oh, and when you come, bring some of those chocolate almonds that you know I like. I don't know why you don't quit that silly job of yours so you'd have more time to take care of things for me. You could easily live on your trust fund—"

Marjorie stopped the machine and took a moment before she turned back to face Jackson. "No bad guys leaving messages," she said with obvious forced lightness as she returned to the table.

"And no trust fund," he replied softly.

This time the smile she offered him had no heart behind it. "Stepfather number two managed to get power of attorney over my trust fund and by the time he left my mother there was nothing left."

"And your mother isn't aware of the fact that you have no money except a paycheck?"

"I've tried to keep her protected as much as possible in financial matters. Besides, it doesn't matter. I'm not exactly the trust-fund-baby type."

"But you could have been," Jackson replied. His stomach twisted with a wave of grief as he saw the residual effects left behind when a con man came to town.

This time her smile was genuine. "No, I could never spend my days buying shoes and fancy dresses and attending charity events. I knew I wanted to be an FBI agent when I was fairly young. I wanted a life of rules and structure. I like having plans and sticking to them, the mundane tasks of filing reports and interviewing suspects."

"But a little spontaneity never hurts. I mean, I'm sure you didn't expect to be thrown on the floor and shot at tonight," he replied.

"I know the unexpected happens on the job, but there's not much room for spontaneity in my personal life, and that's the way I like it. And now, let's firm up our plans for tomorrow."

It was nearly one o'clock in the morning by the time they finished talking and Marjorie carried their cups to the sink. She quickly washed them and placed them on a dish drainer and then turned to look at him. "Since it's so late, why don't we plan on leaving here around nine in the morning?"

"Noon sounds better, but I can do nine," he agreed.

She looked exhausted. Her face had once again taken on a pale cast, and dark shadows rode the delicate skin just beneath her eyes. Her shoulders no longer held rigid tension but rather slumped slightly with the weight of the long day.

As they left the kitchen she turned out the lights and he checked the front door to make sure it was locked up tight. Together they started down the hallway.

"You should find everything you need in the bathroom beneath the sink cabinet," she said as they paused in front of his bedroom. "If you need anything just let me know. Good night, Jackson."

"Good night, Maggie."

She turned to head to her own bedroom, and Jackson realized he couldn't just let her go, not without doing something spontaneous and probably dangerous, as well.

He called her name, and when she turned back to face him, he didn't give himself time to think—he certainly didn't give her a chance to prepare—he simply pulled her into his arms and bent his head to capture her lips with his.

She stiffened and he braced himself for her hands against his chest, pushing him away, or a knee to the groin that would take him down to the carpeting.

But as the kiss continued, she melted into him, became soft and pliant as her arms wound around his neck and tangled in the thick hair at the nape of his neck. The hot, sweet taste of her, the feel of her sexy curves in his arms, was so good it was bad. He knew on every level this was a mistake, but he was unable to deny himself this moment with this particular woman.

She was like nobody else he'd ever kissed before. Her lips were sweeter, her body hotter and he recognized on some elemental level that without trying she was burrowing into his brain, into his heart, where no other woman had ever been before.

This thought halted the kiss. He pulled back and released her and stumbled back a step. She stared at him, a stunned look on her face. She raised a hand and touched her lips with fingers that trembled.

"Why did you do that?" Her voice was husky, and the sound shot a new wave of desire through him.

"Spontaneity," he said. "It's not always a bad thing, even in your personal life."

He didn't wait for her to reply, knew only the need to escape from her before he did something even more stupid. He turned and went into the bedroom and quietly closed the door behind him.

MARJORIE TOSSED AND TURNED for the next couple of hours, cold as she remembered the sounds of the bullets that might have killed them, and heated by Jackson's kiss.

The man definitely knew how to kiss a woman so that her toes curled and desire for more pooled in the pit of her stomach.

The one relationship Marjorie had experienced in her past had lasted only three weeks. He'd been a handsome, slightly quirky computer geek. She'd found his conversation tedious, the sex adequate but nothing mind-blowing, and ultimately had decided what she'd always known: relationships were more trouble than they were worth.

But she had a feeling making love with Jackson might be a mind-blowing experience, not that she intended to allow that to happen. Tomorrow night he would be in another motel room and she wouldn't have to worry…or want any more hallway encounters.

What she needed to focus on was who had tried to kill them and what had happened to Amberly and Cole Caldwell. That was her job, not personal interest in the very hot Southerner who, if she allowed him, just might have the ability to charm her right out of her panties.

She had no idea what time she finally fell asleep, but she awakened to the scent of frying sausage. She frowned. The only food items that had been in her fridge were half a head of lettuce, a couple of eggs and a dozen or so protein bars that helped her get through long days. There had definitely not been any sausage.

She got out of bed, grabbed the clothes she would wear for the day and then skipped from her room into

the bathroom for a quick shower before making an official appearance in the kitchen.

It didn't take her long to shower and dress in her
usual uniform of a white blouse and black slacks, with
her identification clipped to a thin belt around her
waist. She liked the fact that each morning she didn't
have to think about what to wear, that she wasn't the
type of woman to stand in front of a closet and dither
about the daily couture.

Before leaving the bathroom she stared at her reflection in the mirror and reached up to touch her
lips...the lips that Jackson had taken such possession
of the night before.

She wasn't sure what to make of him. She wanted
to believe he was a rake, a smooth-talking scoundrel
who couldn't be trusted except as an efficient partner.
And yet in the brief time she'd known him she'd seen
sides to him that had confused her, made her wonder
what man she might find beneath the easy charm and
sweet talk.

Shaking her head, she left the bathroom, chastising
herself for any thoughts of Jackson the man and determined to think of him only as Jackson her partner.

He was just pulling a tray of hot biscuits from the
oven when she walked into the kitchen. "Ah, perfect
timing," he said with a quick smile. "The sausage is
cooked, the biscuits are done and the gravy is bub-
bly hot."

She noticed he'd already set the table as she walked
to the counter with the coffeepot and poured herself
a cup. "Where did all of this come from?" she asked.

He plucked the biscuits off the baking tray and
placed them on a plate. "Hope you don't mind but I

borrowed your car to head to the nearest grocery store. Once I got up and saw the contents of your pantry and fridge, I knew I was in dire circumstances."

She sat at the table and watched as he poured the gravy into a pitcher and then carried the food to the center of the tiny table.

"Did you know you had fourteen protein bars in there, but nothing fit to eat?" He gestured for her to pick up her fork and dig in. "Maybe you can eat those things, but I need real food, so I stocked both the freezer and the refrigerator."

"You shouldn't have done that," she protested. Those weren't the actions of a man who intended to move into another motel room today. They were the actions of a man who had found his roost and had no intention of leaving it.

"Darlin', I had to do it—it's called self-preservation." He grinned and grabbed his fork. "Now, eat. We've got a long day ahead of us, and breakfast is the most important meal to kick-start your body and brain."

Oh, she was kick-started, all right. As she ate, she tried to stay focused off the kiss they'd shared the night before, and tried to figure out a nice way to kick him out of her house.

By the time they were finished eating and had cleaned up the kitchen, she still hadn't figured it out. Hopefully before the day ended she could make him believe that staying in her place wasn't a good plan.

Before they left the house she called her director, who already had the details of what had happened the night before at the motel and was conducting an internal investigation among the handful of people who knew where Jackson would be staying while in town.

With that issue taken care of, Marjorie and Jackson were on their way to Mystic Lake to begin a new round of questioning. Despite the fact that they'd agreed the night before to be on the road around nine, they got an early start. Neither of them had slept in later than usual.

Their first stop would be Natalie Redwing's place. Although they would arrive there fairly early, around eight-thirty, they hoped to catch the woman off guard.

"You can do the interview with Natalie Redwing," Marjorie said, and gave the handsome man next to her a quick glance. "Maybe some of that smooth charm of yours will work its magic and we'll actually get some answers."

"Sounds like a tough assignment to me," he replied lightly.

She laughed. "Yeah, like breathing." She turned onto the highway that would take them to the little town. "We also need to talk to Deputy Black and see if he's heard any gossip about what went down last night and find out if Jeff Maynard has an alibi for the time of the shooting."

"I've got the names of everyone we need to talk to written down," Jackson assured her. "We'll get them all covered today unless something else comes up. What we need to focus on is watching our backs. Last night was a heads-up that somebody is willing to kill to keep us from gaining answers."

A residual chill swept through Marjorie as she thought of those moments the night before when the world exploded around her and terror had shot through her very soul.

"What happened last night doesn't exactly speak well for Amberly and Cole's well-being," she said, the words painful as they fell from her mouth.

"No, it doesn't," he replied after a moment of hesitation. She was grateful he didn't pretend that the couple was probably just fine and being held captive somewhere for some unknown reason.

If they were correct, in that Amberly and Cole had disappeared on Friday night, then tomorrow marked a full week that they'd been missing. A part of her was already mourning the two and that only made her more determined to find out the who and the why of what had happened to them.

It would have been difficult to drive by Natalie Redwing's mobile home in the trailer park located on the west end of the small town of Mystic Lake without taking notice of it. Painted a brilliant orange, with colorful dream catchers and tinkling chimes hanging down from nails at the top of the built-on wooden porch, it was like a brain freeze to the eyes.

No sooner had they pulled into the driveway than a heavyset Native American stepped out onto the front porch, a shotgun lowered to point to the ground, and a wary frown on her plump face. "Friend or foe?" she asked as Jackson opened his car door but didn't step out.

"Depends on what you do with that shotgun," he replied. "We're FBI and we're here to ask you some questions."

She nodded and propped the gun against the doorframe and motioned them out of the car. "A woman alone can't be too careful these days," she said.

Clad in a yellow-and-turquoise muumuu with bright orange flip-flops, she was as colorful as her home. When they reached her porch, she gestured them into two old wicker chairs while she remained standing. "I suppose you're here about the sheriff and his wife. I figured eventually somebody would be by to talk to me."

"And here we are," Jackson said, and flashed her one of his devastating smiles. Instantly the frown across Natalie's face disappeared.

"Why, aren't you a handsome hunk," she said, her voice taking on a softer, almost simpering quality.

"Thanks, you're a fine-looking lady yourself," he replied. "Unfortunately this is a business visit and not a pleasure one. We need to know about your relationship with Sheriff Caldwell and his wife."

"Cole and I were good friends," she said, her gaze never leaving Jackson's face. Marjorie might just as well have been a pet rock on the porch. "I knew Amberly because we occasionally worked together at the Native American Heritage Center in Kansas City, but we weren't real close." She took a step closer to Jackson and leaned toward him. "I thought she was a little bit snooty, if you know what I mean."

Jackson leaned toward her, as if captivated by anything that might fall out of her mouth. "So, were you upset when the two of them got married? I mean, a good-looking woman like you, maybe you had some plans for yourself with Cole."

"I won't lie, I had visions of me and Cole together at one time." The frown creased her forehead again.

"But once I saw the two of them together it was so obvious that they belonged with each other."

As they spoke the chimes tinkled and clanged riotously in a warm breeze, the cacophony of discordant sound making Marjorie's head ache.

"I know this sounds crazy for a lovely woman like you, but we heard a rumor that you were kind of stalking Cole," Jackson said. He shook a quick glance at Marjorie, who had been watching the two of them intently.

"I was never stalking Cole," Natalie scoffed. "But I suppose somebody might have gotten the wrong impression, because it might have looked like I was stalking them both."

Jackson leaned back in his chair. "And why would you be doing that, sweetheart?"

Natalie walked over to the porch railing and leaned against it, her gaze distant for a moment, and then she focused back on Jackson. "Being Native American, I'm tuned into emotions deeper than other people. It's a gift of my heritage. There was something primal between Amberly and Cole, a force, an energy that proclaimed them soul mates. I liked seeing them together."

"When was the last time you saw them?" Marjorie asked, unable to stay quiet another minute.

"I saw Cole on Thursday, but it had been the weekend before they disappeared that I saw Amberly and him together. They were having dinner together in the local diner and I ate at the counter that night."

"Do you know anyone who might want to hurt them?" Jackson asked.

"Jeff Maynard and his group of idiots weren't too

fond of Cole, but I can't imagine any of them doing something like this. You are going to find them, aren't you? What they had between them was something magical, and it would be a shame if they have somehow been destroyed."

Her words were filled with emotion, and tears slipped down her face. "Watching them together made me feel like I bathed in their love. It made me believe that there was somebody out there who I could connect with on that emotional, sexual, loving level."

She gave a harsh laugh. "I know, I'm just a crazy, lonely fat woman living my life vicariously through others. If you came here to find out if I had anything to do with Amberly and Cole's disappearance, then you've come to the wrong place."

Jackson exchanged glances with Marjorie. Marjorie wasn't sure what to believe. Natalie came across as a straight-shooter, but really good liars had the same ability. Still, she knew they wouldn't get any more pertinent information here, and so she stood, indicating to Jackson that as far as she was concerned they were finished here.

Jackson got up and stood next to her. "We may be back with more questions for you," he said.

Natalie's eyes twinkled. "You can come back here whenever you want, you charming devil, but I have a feeling it would still just be business and not pleasure." Her gaze shot from Jackson to Marjorie and then back again. "I sense more than a little primal energy between the two of you." She smiled slyly. "If I were you two, I'd get after it."

"I'm working on it," Jackson said with a laugh as Marjorie fought both the flaming heat in her cheeks and the desire to punch him in the arm…hard.

Chapter Six

"She sensed something primal between us," Jackson said when they were back in the car and headed to find Jeff Maynard's friend Jimmy Tanner.

"The sound of all those wind chimes has obviously scrambled her brains," Marjorie replied.

Jackson grinned, amused by the straight set of her shoulders, the grim set of her lush lips. "Would it be so bad if there was some primal desire between us?"

"Whether there is or isn't doesn't matter," she replied. "You're just a man who is in town until this case is solved and then you'll go back to Baton Rouge and the bimbos you're accustomed to dating."

"Now, what on earth would make you think I'd date bimbos?" he asked.

"All I want to know from you is what you thought of Natalie Redwing. Do you think she's a harmless stalker or somebody more dangerous?"

Although with the memory of kissing Maggie far too fresh in his mind he'd rather talk about primal need, he gave her a pass. "I'm not sure. I think maybe she's no more than a bit of a voyeur, living her life by stalking people who have what she wants. I'd be more inclined to move her up the suspect list if Amberly was dead and Cole was still alive and here."

"Agreed."

"Still, we'll do a full background check on her and see if anything comes to light."

"Maybe Jimmy Tanner will have some answers for us. We already know that we need to check Jeff Maynard's alibi for the night the Caldwells went missing, and we know he might have a motive, in that the last investigation Amberly and Cole worked on together apparently ended Jimmy's marriage."

"And from what Deputy Black told us, Jimmy is now working as a freelance sort of handyman carpenter. We'll see if we can catch him at home at the motel, otherwise we'll have to see if we can find out where he's working for the day."

He could tell she was grateful that the talk had turned to the case, and he knew that was why he was here, that it should be of utmost importance to him. Amberly and Cole were two people who desperately needed help. Jackson wasn't sure at this point if they'd be found alive or dead, but in either case there were also people who needed closure.

Still, he couldn't deny that in the brief time he'd known Maggie, she'd touched him in places no woman ever had before. She made him want to be a better man than he'd ever been in his life, and she'd made him more ashamed than he'd ever been of where he'd come from.

Jimmy Tanner's current residence was at the Mystic Lake Motel. Jackson sighed with relief as he saw the white panel truck parked out front. A ladder was attached to the roof, and it was obviously a work vehicle. It looked as if Jimmy was home.

The motel didn't appear to be a five-star establishment; rather it looked as if it would have to struggle to make two-star status.

Seeing the broken windows of one unit, an old rusty sports car parked nearby, Jackson got out of the car with his hand on the butt of his gun.

The place smelled like danger...like drug deals and hookers and an alcoholic's oasis. It held the scent of crime and lawlessness, and he was glad to see that his partner had the same vibe, for her hand was on the butt of her gun, as well.

They exchanged sober glances as they approached the end unit that belonged to Jimmy. The curtains were drawn over the filthy windows, making it impossible for them to get a glimpse of what they might face when the door opened.

Jackson knocked on the door, tensed as he waited for a response. Marjorie stood on the opposite side of the entrance, her features also taut and sober.

There was no reply. He knocked again, harder this time, certain that Jimmy the handyman was hiding out inside. His suspicion was confirmed when the curtain at the window moved slightly and then fell back into place.

"He's in there," Jackson said softly to Maggie. He banged on the door once again. "Jimmy Tanner, come outside." Before he could identify them as FBI agents, a crash of glass sounded from around the back of the building.

"He's running," Maggie said, and together she and Jackson took off around the side of the building.

The back of the motel was nothing but a field of weeds, and in the distance were two things: the glittering water of the lake for which the town had been named, and a brown-haired man clad in jeans and a white T-shirt running away as fast as his legs could carry him.

"Halt!" Jackson yelled as he raced to catch him. The last thing he wanted was a damned footrace in this heat and humidity.

He was vaguely surprised that Maggie was matching him step for step. Not only sexy, but fast, he thought with admiration.

"Hey, Jimmy," she yelled. "If you don't stop running, then I'm going to shoot you." Maggie stopped in place and pulled her gun from her holster and assumed a shooter stance.

Jimmy glanced backward, his eyes wild with fear, and his feet skidded to a halt. He slowly turned to face them, with his hands above his head. "If she's paid you to shoot me, then just get it over with," he exclaimed. "She's taken everything else from me, she might as well get my life, too."

As Maggie and Jackson drew nearer, Jackson noticed that one of Jimmy's eyes held the faint yellow bruising of a healing black eye, and his lower lip was scabbed over as if he'd taken a beating in the past week or so.

"Who is 'she'?"

"My ex-wife. Aren't you just two more goons she hired to beat the hell out of me?"

"Do I look like a goon who's going to beat the hell out of you?" Maggie asked.

"You never know," Jimmy replied. "My ex is crazy enough to hire some woman just to get me off guard."

"Actually, we're FBI agents, you dumb ass, and we'd like to ask you some questions," Jackson replied. The late July sun was hot, and Jackson was in no mood to conduct an interview in the middle of a field. "We can do this back at your place or we can take you into the sheriff's office. Your choice."

"My place," he replied. "I try not to show my face around the sheriff's station. Just looking at the building makes me want to punch Cole Caldwell upside the head."

They began walking back toward the motel. "Is this about the sheriff's disappearance?" he asked.

"Partly," Jackson replied.

Jimmy eyed him with narrow eyes. "I might have a reason to want to punch Cole in the chin, but really all he did was confirm to my wife what she'd known for years, that I'd been cheating on her all along. For some reason Tara finally went crazy on me. She divorced me, took most everything I owned and has been hiring thugs to beat me up on a regular basis."

By that time they'd reached the front of his motel room. He opened the door and gestured them inside. The space was surprisingly clean, with the bed neatly made and a suitcase half-packed on the floor.

"Packing or unpacking?" Jackson asked as he thumbed a finger at the suitcase.

"Somewhere in between." Jimmy sank down on the edge of the bed while Jackson and Marjorie remained standing just inside the door. "As soon as I get enough money together I'm heading out of this town. I want to get as far away from Tara as I possibly can, but I'm sure you aren't here because of my marital issues."

"We're here to check on an alibi for the time of the disappearance of Sheriff Caldwell and his wife. Jeff Maynard told us that last Friday night, you, Raymond Chandler and he were all here playing poker."

Jimmy rubbed a hand across his sweaty forehead. "You know, a month ago I would have saved his sorry butt by lying for him. But I'm not lying for anyone anymore, and I just want to keep my nose clean and get out of town as soon as possible. Ray and I met here for our usual poker night, but Jeff never showed up. The two of us were here until about one in the morning, playing two-handed card games and drinking beer."

Jimmy's features hardened. "I'm not in the mood to tell you something that isn't true. The three of us have been jokes in this town, losers and cheaters and low-lifes, but I'm turning things around and I don't want to start by lying to Feds."

Jackson exchanged a look with Marjorie. "Then it appears we need to speak to Jeff again."

"I won't lie, I didn't like Cole, but Jeff hated him. I hope he isn't crazy enough to do something stupid, but you never know, where Jeff is concerned, especially if he's been drinking," Jimmy said. "He gets stupid when he gets drunk."

Marjorie pulled one of her cards from her purse and handed it to Jimmy. "Don't leave town without letting us know your plans."

He nodded, and moments later Jackson and Marjorie were back in the car. "I've got to tell you, Maggie girl, you definitely look hot in a shooter stance."

She shot him the look of aggravation he expected, and he laughed.

"I don't know what you find so funny. We're spinning our wheels here and going nowhere fast in this investigation."

"Not true," he protested. "We just found out that Jeff Maynard lied about his alibi. I'd say that's a break for us."

"But everyone we've talked to about him has told us he's not very bright," she replied. "And whoever got Cole and Amberly out of their house in the middle of the night had to be smart."

"Jeff just might be hiding his cunning under a barrel." Jackson thought of the surly bartender. "We'll check him out and then we'll head back to Kansas City. We'll pick up some of those chocolates your mother likes and then take them to her and have a little visit."

She shot him a startled look. "That's not necessary. She can wait until I can get time to visit her alone."

"On the contrary. I'd love an opportunity to chat with dear old Mom," he replied.

He was interested to meet her mother, to find out what kind of a woman would allow herself to be fleeced out of not just her own fortune but her daughter's, as well.

He also found himself wondering what Marjorie's bedroom looked like. If there was a touch of luxury there that wasn't present in the rest of her tiny house. Did she indulge herself in colorful silk sheets or wear an expensive nightgown to bed every night?

He pulled his thoughts back into the case, knowing that it didn't matter if Natalie Redwing had sensed something primal between him and Maggie. It didn't matter that he felt it himself—not just desire, but also need. Not just a sexual pull but an emotional one, as well. None of it mattered, because he knew they would never follow through on it.

The case—he had to remain focused on the case. He needed to find the answers, solve the case and get back home before Maggie got any deeper into his skin.

UNFORTUNATELY THE SHORT DRIVE to Bledsoe's tavern was a waste of time. It was Jeff's night off.

They spent an hour driving around town, trying to chase down his whereabouts, but finally gave up and headed back to Kansas City.

The last thing Marjorie wanted was to take Jackson to her mother's apartment. There was no reason for the two of them to ever meet, no reason for Jackson to invade her personal life to such a degree.

And yet she knew she should probably stop by for a quick visit now. With the information about the lying Jeff Maynard on the table before them she had a feeling the case was about to take on a life of its own and time to visit with her mother might not come again for a while.

It took her only minutes to stop at the specialty store that sold the expensive white-and-dark-chocolate almonds that her mother loved, and then she was back in the car with Jackson and headed to the upscale apartment building where her mother lived.

"You look nervous," Jackson observed.

She frowned and released a sigh. "I guess I just don't want you to judge my mother as some silly ninny who just lets men scam her. My father spoiled her. He took care of the finances and when he died she'd never paid a bill in her life. She was utterly clueless. If she has any faults at all, it's that she trusted too much and trusted the wrong men."

"Maggie, you don't have to defend your mother to me." Jackson's voice was a low, gentle caress. "Trust me, I'm the last person to judge anyone."

She felt herself relax a bit. "No matter what man was in her life at the time, she always made me feel like I was her top priority. Despite everything she was a good and loving mother to me."

"You never wanted kids?" he asked.

A tiny ache shot off in her heart. "In another world, in another life, I might have wanted children. But, considering the fact that I don't want a man in my life, I made the decision that children were out of the question."

She glanced at him, her heart doing a small leap as always at his attractiveness. "You know so much about my early life, but I don't know much about yours."

"There really isn't much to tell. I don't have any memories of my mother, and my dad was kind of a vagabond. We moved around a lot."

His voice held a stress it hadn't before, and it immediately gave her the feeling that there was more to the story than the tiny bit he'd just shared.

"Are you and your father close?" she asked, wanting more details of who he was and where he'd come from.

"No." The single word snapped out of him like a gunshot. He raised a hand and raked it through his thick hair. "We had a falling-out years ago and went our separate ways."

She shot him another glance and he gave her his irreverent, sexy smile. "I'm just a poor, lonely Southern boy with nobody meaningful to fill up the hours of my days and nights."

"I have a feeling that's just the way you like it," she returned. When she cast him another surreptitious glance, he was staring out the passenger window.

She suspected there was a great depth inside him, a place where he allowed nobody to go. A part of her wanted to be invited in, wanted to discover the man beneath the charm, but it was a foolish wish that would lead only to making their parting more difficult when it came time for him to leave and return to his home in Baton Rouge.

As she pulled into a space in the parking lot in front of her mother's apartment building, nervous anxiety tingled through her veins.

She knew it was past time for her to visit with her mother, but it felt strange to have Jackson along with her. They got out of the car and approached the double doors where an intercom was used as security.

She punched the button to contact her mother, who buzzed them in to the small lobby. "Mom's place is on the second floor," she said as she led him toward the nearby elevator. "Her name is Katherine, Katherine Devoe."

They stepped into the elevator and instantly she was aware that he was too male, too close, and the memory of that kiss they'd shared seared through her brain.

"We'll keep this brief," she said as she tightened her fingers on the box of chocolate.

"Whatever," he agreed easily. "We can't do much more about the investigation until morning. Jeff Maynard is my top priority at the moment, and we already know he won't be in at the tavern until late tomorrow afternoon."

The elevator stopped and the doors slid open. If she were smart, she'd make this visit with her mother last until bedtime. It was obvious Jackson intended to bunk with her another night. He'd made no other arrangements to go anywhere else throughout the day.

It was just after six now, and that left far too many evening hours spent in Jackson's company before bedtime. *We'll talk about the case,* she told herself as she rapped on her mother's apartment door.

Katherine Devoe was an older, taller version of Marjorie. She had the same red-blond hair, the same green eyes, and as she opened the door, those eyes lit up with delight.

"Marjorie," she exclaimed, and pulled Marjorie into a quick hug. She released her, her gaze lingering on Jackson, who stood just behind Marjorie. "I see you not only brought me a box of chocolates, but some eye candy, as well."

"Jackson Revannaugh," he said and held out his hand. Katherine slipped her hand into his and released a girlish giggle as Jackson lowered his mouth to kiss the back of her hand. "It's a real pleasure to meet the mother of such an amazing woman," he said as he released Katherine's hand. "I see now where Maggie gets her looks."

"Maggie?" Katherine raised a perfectly waxed eyebrow. "I like it."

He was definitely pouring it on thick, Marjorie thought as she beelined for the white sofa. Jackson followed, sitting far too close to her.

Katherine closed and locked the door and then

turned to face them, delight on her pretty features. "Well, isn't this a special night." She gazed at Jackson. "My daughter has never brought a friend to visit."

"He's not a friend, he's my partner," Marjorie exclaimed.

"Well, then, you've never brought a partner over to visit, either," Katherine said. "May I get either of you something to drink?"

"I'm fine," Marjorie replied.

"I don't suppose you have any bourbon?" Jackson asked.

Katherine flew to the glass-and-gold minibar in the corner of the room. "I do have some bourbon. Straight up or on the rocks?"

"Straight up is fine." He leaned back on the sofa, looking as relaxed as if he'd been here a hundred times before.

"I do believe I hear a little of the good old South in your accent, Mr. Revannaugh," Katherine said as she fixed the drink.

"Born in Baton Rouge and spent most of my time in and around the area," he replied as she handed him the drink.

"What a coincidence—I had a visitor yesterday who was from Baton Rouge. He told me he'd moved up to Mystic Lake to retire."

Every nerve in Marjorie's body jangled with adrenaline. "That is quite a coincidence," Jackson replied. "An old friend of yours?"

"Actually, I'd never met the man before in my life, but he said he was an old friend of Big Bob, my second husband. He was a very nice man, and we had a pleasant visit."

"What was his name?" Marjorie's nerves refused to quiet.

Katherine frowned for a moment. "Edward...Edward Benson— No that isn't right. Bentz. Edward Bentz, that's it."

Marjorie made a mental note of the name as Jackson and her mother visited while he sipped on his drink. It was obvious that Katherine was utterly charmed by Jackson, who was on his best behavior and regaled the older woman with stories of old cases along with his admiration for Marjorie.

Katherine was lapping it up, smiling with motherly approval at Marjorie, as if pleased that her daughter had finally found such a wonderful man.

They wound up staying for an hour, then Marjorie was the one to call a halt to the visit. "Mom, we've still got to grab some dinner and do some work," she said as she stood.

"Your daughter is a tough taskmaster," Jackson said teasingly as he also got up from the sofa.

"She is all about work, but I keep telling her that life shouldn't be just about that." Katherine's eyes twinkled at Jackson, as if she shared a secret with him. "Maybe you can make her slow down a bit and enjoy the fun in life."

"Mom can simper and you can wink all you want, but nobody is going to make me change," Marjorie said once they were alone in the elevator and headed back downstairs.

"It's obvious your mother has your best interests at heart," he replied.

"Whatever," she said as they exited the elevator.

She didn't speak again until they were in the car and headed to her house.

"Something isn't right." Worry simmered in the pit of her stomach.

"Something isn't right about what?" he asked.

"Big Bob was from Texas, not from the South. I'd like to know what a man from Baton Rouge who has just recently moved to the small town of Mystic Lake is doing visiting with my mother."

"Does seem like a bit of a coincidence," Jackson replied, his voice low and heavy with a new somber note.

"I don't know about you, but I'm not much of a believer when it comes to those kinds of coincidences. We need to find Edward Bentz and see what he's up to. I have a bad feeling and I want to make sure that somehow something we're working on now hasn't brought danger to my mother's doorstep."

She swallowed hard, but it was impossible to get the taste of something bad about to happen out of her throat.

Chapter Seven

Jackson paced the floor of Maggie's tiny kitchen, fighting the frustration of three long days without answers, and a simmering desire for the woman that threatened to explode out of control at any given moment.

For the past three days they'd been chasing down people they couldn't find. Jeff Maynard either had skipped town or was holed up with somebody they didn't know about.

According to his boss at Bledsoe's, Jeff had called and asked for a few days off due to a bad case of the flu. Jackson suspected he had a bad case of FBI-itis. Eventually he'd poke his head out or somebody in town would slip up, and they'd find him.

Edward Bentz had also been an elusive character. They'd discovered he was renting a room from an older woman named Betty Fields. They'd checked with her only to discover that Edward had gone back to Baton Rouge to finish up some last-minute business and would be back at her place late that evening.

Jackson had checked with his contacts in Baton Rouge to get a handle on the man, but apparently he had no criminal record and a background search had yielded only the information that he was fifty-five years old, had worked for over twenty years distributing medical supplies in and around the Baton Rouge area and several other states, and had recently retired from that position.

Unbeknownst to Maggie, Jackson had contacted her director and arranged for an agent to sit outside Katherine Devoe's apartment as security until they had an opportunity to check out Edward Bentz.

Meanwhile, nothing had come of the investigation into the shoot-out at the motel except that whoever had fired the shots had indeed used an Uzi…serious firepower that was definitely intended to kill.

He poured himself a cup of coffee and flopped in one of the two chairs at the table. The sun was just beginning to peek up shy, faint beams over the horizon.

Although they had been unable to connect with the two people they most wanted to speak to, the hours of the days hadn't passed with inactivity. Yesterday they'd spent the entire day in the Mystic Lake sheriff's office, interviewing every single person who had worked under Cole's command.

They'd learned that Cole was considered a tough but fair boss. While some of the deputies seemed to have a healthy fear of Cole, it was tempered with an enormous amount of respect. No red flags had presented, leaving Marjorie and Cole to come home each day still confused about who was behind whatever had happened to Amberly and Cole.

It bothered him that they hadn't found their bodies. It was just like the case he'd been working on in Bachelor Moon, where Sam and his wife and their daughter had been missing now for weeks, and their bodies had never been found. The case remained unsolved.

He and Maggie had fallen into a routine, and he knew he probably had about half an hour before she'd make her morning appearance in the kitchen.

Maggie. He took another sip of his coffee and closed his eyes. He had yet to see her bedroom, but last night in the middle of the night they'd accidently bumped into each other in the hallway. The tiny night-light she kept plugged into the socket next to the bathroom had been enough illumination for him to see that she'd been clad in a short deep purple silk nightgown that had fired the red in her hair and showcased every curve she possessed.

Jackson had nearly fallen to his knees with desire. Their eyes had locked in the dim hallway, hers gleaming with a light that made him want to reach out, to pick her up in his arms and carry her into a bedroom and make love to her.

But before he'd been able to move a muscle, she'd scampered like a rabbit back into her bedroom and closed the door behind her.

He'd had a feeling that if they'd remained in that hallway for a second longer, she would have awakened in his arms this morning after a long night of lovemaking.

He blew out a sigh of frustration, both mental and sexual. He felt like a powder keg about to explode. Taking another drink of his coffee, he smelled her before she entered the room, that sweet floral scent that ramped up his testosterone to caveman levels.

"Well, aren't we informal today," she said as she entered the kitchen and her gaze took in his jeans and white polo shirt.

"Yeah, with this heat I didn't feel like doing the

whole agent kind of dress code." He gazed at her navy slacks and white blouse. "You know, you could do casual with me…maybe some shorts and a blouse that actually has some color to it. I have to admit, you look amazing in purple."

He grinned as she ignored him and strode over to the coffeepot. "You can pretend you didn't hear me, but the flames in your cheeks tell me otherwise."

"A gentleman would never mention a lady's nightgown," she replied.

Jackson laughed. "I don't remember ever confessing to be a hundred percent gentleman, and do you realize how often you blush?" He waited until she was seated across from him at the table. "Are you a virgin?"

She slapped a hand across her mouth in an obvious effort to prevent herself from spewing coffee. She swallowed and coughed, all the while glaring at him with those amazing green eyes. "Not that it's any of your business, but no, I'm not a virgin. Why are you even thinking about things like that?"

There was a new wariness in her eyes that told him to back off. He wrapped his hands around his coffee cup and shrugged. "Because I figured it was easier than thinking about this damn case. If it wasn't for that shooting at the motel, I'd be feeling more than a little bit of déjà vu."

"What do you mean?" She was obviously relieved by the change in topic.

"If Cole and Amberly were kidnapped, then so far we haven't figured out a motive. In the case I was working on in Bachelor Moon, we never figured out a motive for what we finally came to believe had to have been a kidnapping. In both cases no ransom notes have been received, everyone couldn't imagine the people having any enemies and no bodies have been found."

"But you said none of the investigators in the case in Bachelor Moon were threatened in any way," she replied, obviously not wanting the cases to be related and still clinging to the hope that they would find the couple alive and well any day now.

"True," he replied. Hell, he didn't want the two cases to be related, but comparing the facts of the crimes gave him pause. The fact that Edward Bentz was from the Baton Rouge area, which was very close to Bachelor Moon, and that he was now in Mystic Lake definitely was too much of a coincidence to ignore.

He got up from the table and headed toward the fridge. "I'll scramble us up some eggs and make toast and then we can get on the road. Hopefully today we'll get some answers that will help make something about this case come into focus."

Breakfast was eaten quickly, with the conversation centered on their visit with Marjorie's mother. "She's a lovely lady," Jackson said.

"She's got a lot of heart."

"It bothers me that you live like a pauper and she's in that luxury two-bedroom apartment," he admitted.

"I don't live like a pauper," she protested.

He raised a dark brow and held her gaze. "Maggie, I know about what you make for a salary and it's obvious you aren't spending any of it on creature comforts for yourself. Hell, since I've been here I've never even seen you in anything but that white blouse and slacks. Do you have any other wardrobe?"

"Of course I do. I'm fine the way things are. I like helping out my mother."

Jackson finished the last of the eggs on his plate and then looked at her again. "But wouldn't it be better if you'd tell your mother the truth of the situation? Have her move to a place that's more within her means and ease some of the pressure off you?"

"I think we need to solve this case, and you should keep your nose out of my personal life." She straightened in her chair and he knew he'd crossed a line with her.

He reached out his hand and covered one of hers. She tried to pull away, but he held tight. "I just want more for you, Maggie. You deserve more from life."

Her gaze searched his, as if seeking a joke, a facade of charm, but he knew she'd find nothing like that there. He'd spoken the simple, stark truth.

She tried to pull her hand from his again, and this time he let go, and she looked down at her plate. "I appreciate your concern for me, Jackson, but I'm doing just fine. I don't require a lot to be happy."

"Are you happy?" he asked.

Her beautiful green eyes met his once again and a frown darted across her forehead. She took a sip of her coffee and then placed the cup back on the table.

"I never really look for happy. I'm satisfied.... Most of the time I'm content with my life, and that's good enough for me," she finally replied.

He nodded, although he wasn't sure why it wasn't good enough for him. He wanted her to have things—scented oils for a bubble bath, a silk purple dress with killer high heels. She deserved dinner in a candlelit restaurant where the prices weren't on the menu. He wanted her to have a luxurious carpet to rub her bare toes in at the end of a long day, a sofa soft enough to cradle her as she watched television to unwind.

He also wanted her to have laughter, and a man who loved her more than anyone else on the face of the earth. There was no question that she'd suffered financial devastation at the hands of scamming stepfathers, but he imagined she wasn't even aware of the emotional trauma that had gone along with it.

She needed a man who could break through her defenses, a man who could find her pain and heal it with a well of endless love. But he knew he wasn't that man, could never be that man no matter how much he might want to be.

She was right. The best thing he could do was help her solve this crime, and keep his nose out of her personal life. Surely when he was back home in his own apartment, living the superficial personal life he'd built for himself, he'd forget all about a green-eyed beauty who had somehow managed to touch the places in his heart he'd thought were untouchable.

"Don't you find it strange that John Merriweather's ex-wife has been missing for a week and a half and we haven't received one single phone call from him?" Jackson asked as they got into her car. "I mean, if my ex-wife were missing, and we were amicable, I'd be camped out on the doorstep of the head investigator and demanding answers every minute of each day."

"Maybe before we head to Mystic Lake we should have another check-in with John," she suggested.

"Sounds like a plan to me," he agreed.

Marjorie backed out of the driveway and hoped that the day forced her to keep her attention on the case and not on Jackson. The touch of his hand on hers, the genuine emotion she'd seen shining from his eyes at the table had both stunned her and sent a yearning through her she'd never felt before.

She didn't care about expensive furniture or luxury items, but as she'd gazed into those blue eyes of his, she'd wanted him.

She headed in the direction of the Merriweather ranch house and tried not to think of that moment in time when the depth of her yearning for Jackson Revannaugh had taken her breath away, made her tingle with crazy need.

She realized that a part of her wouldn't be averse to making love to him…just once, knowing that it would never mean anything, that she wouldn't see him as a threat to the single life she'd chosen for herself.

He had a home to go back to and she had a life to live here. He was probably a great candidate for a single night of hot, mind-blowing sex because she knew they would never mean anything more than that to each other.

As she pulled into John's driveway, she mentally shook herself, needing to get sex and Jackson off her brain and work the case that had gone nowhere so far.

It was strange that John hadn't contacted anyone since Amberly's disappearance. Surely, even though he was her ex-husband, it would be normal, since he and Amberly shared a child, for him to be rattling cages to find her. So why wasn't he?

She didn't realize how early it was until the door opened and a young boy with jet-black hair and big brown eyes answered. John was behind him in a second. "Any news?" he asked as he ushered the two of them inside.

"We have a few leads we're following," Jackson replied.

Marjorie sat on the sofa, and Max sidled up next to her. "Are you looking for my mom and Daddy Cole?" He leaned into her, bringing with him the scent of soap and innocence that shot a stab of pain straight through Marjorie. This was the victim of whatever had happened, a little boy who desperately needed his mommy back where she belonged.

"We're trying our very best to find them," she replied, fighting her impulse to wrap him in her arms.

"You haven't heard anything?" Jackson asked, his features set in stern lines, reminding Marjorie that he still believed John was their number one suspect.

"Nothing," John replied, his voice holding misery. "I've reached out to all her friends, people she'd mentioned working with, anyone I can think of, but nobody knows anything about what's happened."

He sank down in a chair and motioned Max to his side. "I've been making her welcome-home cards," Max said. "But I need her to come home so I can give them to her."

"We're doing our best to make that happen," Marjorie said. Max nodded, his expression far too somber and grown-up for such a little boy.

"We were just wondering why we hadn't heard from you," Jackson said, his gaze still focused on John.

John shrugged. "I haven't contacted you because I don't have any information to help you. I'd much rather you spend your time working on finding them than talking to me." He raised his chin slightly, as if he felt Jackson's suspicion. "If it would make you feel better about me, I'll start calling you six or seven times a day for a progress report."

Jackson's jaw clenched. "I don't think that's necessary. We'll keep you informed of any new developments, and you let us know if you learn anything that might be helpful." His glance at Marjorie indicated he was ready to leave.

As Marjorie stood up, Max returned to her side. "When you find my mom, would you please bring her home as soon as possible?" His dark eyes filled with tears. "I miss her really, really bad."

Again her heart squeezed painfully tight as she placed a hand gently on his shoulder. "We're doing the best we can, Max."

He nodded and stepped back to his father's side. "We'll be in touch," Jackson said.

Once they were back in the car Marjorie slammed the steering wheel with the palm of her hand. "Who would be so evil to take away that little boy's mother?"

"Let's hope we get some answers in Mystic Lake today," Jackson said, a hint of emotion thickening his voice.

They didn't speak again until they reached the small town. The first place they stopped was at the sheriff's office, where they found Roger Black seated in Cole's office.

"Any news on the missing Jeff Maynard?" Jackson asked the middle-aged head deputy.

"Actually, I have a tip from the rumor mill that he's holed up with Tara Tanner."

Marjorie looked at him in surprise. "Jimmy's ex-wife?"

Roger nodded. "That's the word out on the streets.

Apparently they were seen together last night at the liquor store."

Marjorie's head spun as she remembered their talk with Jimmy. Had Jimmy lied about Jeff not being at the poker party because he was ticked that Jeff was with his ex-wife?

Roger shoved a piece of paper toward them. "This is Tara's address. Be careful—she's a bit of a firecracker."

"So we've heard," Jackson replied.

Roger looked tired, with dark circles beneath his eyes and his brown hair standing on end as if it had felt the rake of frustrated hands through it too many times.

"I wish somebody would find Cole. This job was his, not mine. He's a good sheriff and everyone wants him back behind this desk, where he belongs."

"Right now we have three people in our sights as potential suspects," Marjorie said. "Hopefully in the next hour or so we can either remove Jeff from that short list or confirm that he had something to do with Cole and his wife's disappearance."

"I wish all of us could be more help," Roger said as he stood. "I've got all my men out on the streets, pounding the pavement in an effort to find some kind of answers, but so far we've come up empty-handed on our end."

"We're going to check in with good old Jeff now, and then we have another person of interest we intend to check out this afternoon," Jackson said. "And in between those interviews we'll be walking the streets, as well, seeing what scuttlebutt we might be able to pick up."

"As you both know, we're at your disposal at any time. Whatever you need from us, you've got," Roger replied.

With that Marjorie and Jackson left with directions

to Tara Tanner's house. "Jimmy was mad at Cole for outing his cheating. I wonder what Tara's feelings are about Cole?"

"She should probably consider he did her a big favor," Jackson replied. "I've never understood women who put up with men who cheat on them."

"Maybe it's a matter of a bad man is better than no man at all," she replied.

"I'll bet you wouldn't put up with a cheater," he said.

"You've got that right. If by some miracle, at any point in my life I would decide I wanted a meaningful relationship with a man, I'd expect monogamy. I'd far rather be alone than just have a male body in my life who wasn't committed to me body, heart and soul."

"Apparently Tara Tanner has an addiction to bad boys, if she's moved on from Jimmy to Jeff," Jackson replied.

"We're about to find out," Marjorie replied as she pulled into the driveway of a neat ranch house.

Together they got out of the car and approached the front door. Remembering Roger's warning about Tara being a firecracker, and the fact that it was possible Tara had hired men to beat up Jimmy, Marjorie made sure her gun was easily accessible, if needed.

Jackson knocked on the door and they waited. When there was no reply, he knocked again, harder this time. "Hold your damn horses," a husky female voice called from inside the house.

The door flew open to reveal a bleached blonde wrapped in a red silk robe that had several cigarette burns down the front. The air that wafted out of the door smelled of stale smoke and booze and dirty clothes.

"Yeah? What do you want?" Tara pulled a cigarette

and lighter from the pocket of her robe, lit up and blew smoke at both of them.

"We're here to talk to Jeff," Jackson said.

Tara frowned in fake confusion. "Jeff who?"

"Are we really going to play that game?" Marjorie asked dryly.

A tall shadow appeared behind Tara, and as he came into view he gave them a guilty smile. "Hey," Jeff said.

"We need to talk to you," Marjorie said.

"I figured as much."

Tara stepped back with a shrug of her shoulders, and Jeff gestured them into the semidark living room. Marjorie and Jackson stood just inside the door, looking at the bartender who was dressed only in a pair of plaid boxers and a stained white T-shirt. He wore bed-head badly, and it was obvious they had awakened them.

"Tara, put some coffee on," he said, and she scurried out of the living room.

"None for us," Marjorie replied. She wasn't about to put her mouth on anything that came from this house.

"It's for me," Jeff replied. "We went on a little bender last night and I have a headache from hell. So, guess you're here about the poker party on the night that Cole and his wife disappeared."

"Your alibi sucks, buddy," Jackson said. "Your friends say you never showed up that night. You didn't even call them to say you weren't coming."

Jeff raked a hand through his hair, making his bed-head even worse. "Yeah, well, I hooked up with Tara that night and I couldn't exactly call Jimmy and tell him I was boffing his ex-wife. That was the first night Tara and I hooked up, and I've been here ever since."

Tara came back into the room. "He's telling the truth."

"And we should believe a woman who has been hiring thugs to beat up her ex-husband?" Marjorie said.

Tara's cheeks grew dusky with color. "I don't know what you're talking about." She averted her gaze to the wall.

"I think you do, and we could take you in right now and have you arrested for conspiracy to commit bodily harm or even attempted murder." Marjorie glared at the woman.

Tara's gaze shot back to Marjorie. She folded her arms across her chest, a mutinous expression on her face. "Okay, so maybe I wanted Jimmy to get banged up a little for all the hurt he caused me over the years, but I didn't want him hurt too bad."

Jeff looked at her with stunned surprise. "You actually hired people to beat up Jimmy?"

"It doesn't matter what I did, I'm telling the truth when I say that Jeff was with me on the night that the sheriff and his wife disappeared," Tara said.

She took a deep drag of her cigarette, ignoring the ashes that fell on her ample breasts. "Besides, no offense, but Jeff is too much of a dumb ass to pull off the kidnapping of two people. He couldn't even figure out that it was smart to tell the truth about where he was that night."

"Hey," Jeff said in protest. "I'm not a dumb ass."

Yeah, he was, Marjorie thought and there was no way in hell she'd believe that he had anything to do with whatever had happened at Cole's house almost two weeks ago.

She looked at Jackson. "I think we're done here."

He nodded and inched toward the door as if he couldn't wait to escape the confines of the house. "If we have more questions we'll be in touch. Make sure you both are available," he said.

"Whew, I couldn't wait to get out of there," Jackson said once they were back in the car.

"Did you see the look on Jeff's face when he found out that Tara had hired people to beat up Jimmy?" She laughed. "I don't see a happy ending for Jeff with Tara." Her laughter lasted only a moment and then she sobered. "I also don't think Jeff had anything to do with Cole and Amberly's disappearance. I think we need to take him off our short list of suspects."

A wave of discouragement swept through her. Their list of suspects was dismally small for the length of time they'd been working the case.

For the first time since she'd been handed the case she began to wonder if they'd find the answer they sought, or if this would wind up being like what Jackson had been working on in Bachelor Moon...an unsolved case with collateral damage in the teary eyes of a young child.

Chapter Eight

After leaving Tara's house, Maggie parked her car on the street in front of a business that sold knickknacks and trinkets, and they took off walking.

The heat was unrelenting, the humidity like a sauna, and Jackson wasn't sure what he hoped would happen as they interacted with some of the people of the small town, but he knew with certainty that the investigation was in trouble.

Cell phones had yielded no clues; the bank accounts and credit card activity had remained untouched. It was as if Cole Caldwell and his wife had been levitated into an awaiting spaceship. Just like Sam and Daniella and Macy from Bachelor Moon. He shook his head to dispel the thought.

It was important they continue to work this case by itself until the time came that they either found some answers or had to reach the horrible conclusion that somehow, someway, the Bachelor Moon crime and this one were related.

He shouldn't be confused by attempting to combine the two cases together even though so far they had only one person who had motive for getting rid of Amberly—and that was her ex-husband.

At the moment he was attempting to focus on the chicken fried steak dinner in front of him. He and Maggie had ducked into the diner twenty minutes ago for a late lunch.

Maggie picked at her salad as if without appetite, and he knew the lack of forward motion in the case was affecting her, as well.

"Don't look so depressed," he told her.

She looked up and offered him a small smile. "I just can't get Max's little face out of my head."

As he had that morning, he reached across the table and covered her smaller hand with his. He liked touching her. He wanted to give her comfort, but he knew as far as the case went, he had no words of support to offer her.

She surprised him by twining her fingers with his. "We're doing the best we can, right?" she said.

"Maggie, honey, we're doing everything humanly possible."

She squeezed his fingers a little tighter. "I just don't understand why we haven't found their bodies yet. Deep in my heart I can't imagine a kidnapper keeping them alive for this length of time. That takes planning and work, and even though John might have the best motive for something happening to Amberly, I also believe it would be in his best interest just to kill them and let them be found." She finally pulled her hand away from his.

"He has a lot of resources," Jackson said. "Despite his modest home, he's a very wealthy man. He may have properties we don't even know about, people working for him who aren't even here in town. I've got people from your field office trying to dig deeper into John's life and finances."

She looked at him in surprise. "Working behind your partner's back?"

He shook his head. "Just using whatever resources are available. I know your gut instinct is that John had nothing to do with whatever happened, and to tell you the truth, my gut instinct has completely stopped talking to me. I'm starting to believe in aliens abducting people for scientific studies."

He was rewarded with one of her infrequent but charming laughs. "If that's the case then maybe both of us need to make some aluminum foil antennae to make contact with the alien species."

He grinned. "I think you'd look beautiful in a pair of aluminum earpieces."

"Stop that," she chided him.

"Stop what?"

"Don't flirt with me. I want to know the real Jackson Revannaugh, not the superficial one who spews compliments like the peeing boy statue sprays water."

"I can't believe you just compared me to a little boy statue in Brussels," he said with a laugh. "And just for your information, that wasn't a superficial compliment. That one came straight from my heart."

Her gaze held his and then she looked down and stabbed a piece of carrot with more force than necessary. "You make me a little bit crazy," she said.

"I think you're making me a little crazy, too," he admitted.

They finished their meal in silence and then once again hit the sidewalks for more interaction with the locals. Edward Bentz's landlady, Betty, had told them that she expected Edward back around dinnertime.

Jackson was eager to talk to the man who had ties to both Baton Rouge and Mystic Lake, a man who had visited Maggie's mother before he'd left town.

Certainly, there were elements of this case Jackson found quite troubling, elements that weren't like what he'd investigated with the Bachelor Moon disappearance.

Everything that could be done was being done, both at the federal and at the local levels. There was nothing more they could do but what they were doing.

They spent the next couple of hours going in and out of stores, chatting up people about the sheriff and his wife. Everywhere they went, everyone they spoke to had only good things to say about Cole and Amberly.

Spinning wheels, he thought in disgust. They were hamsters running as fast as they could and getting nowhere. Somebody had been threatened by them, but who? Who had been holding on to the Uzi that shot up their motel room?

He believed the threat had come from this small, pleasant town with its sparkling lake and friendly people. He believed that whoever had shot the gun had followed them from here with the intent to kill them both.

At five o'clock they headed back to Marjorie's car. "I'm hot and my feet are killing me," Marjorie said as she leaned against the driver door. "I'm not used to doing this kind of pounding-the-sidewalk investigation."

"I told you it might be a good day to go casual," Jackson replied, although his feet were aching, too, and his polo shirt was damp with perspiration.

The sun was relentless and the humidity was like a living entity trying to suffocate him to death. "Is it always this humid here?" he asked as he slid into the passenger seat and she got behind the steering wheel.

"This feels worse than usual. I heard somebody say we're supposed to get storms tonight. The atmosphere is definitely soupy enough for them." She started the car and turned the air conditioner on high blast.

It blew hot air for several seconds and then began to cool. Jackson moved his vents to shoot on his face and neck and looked out the window where the sky remained cloudless. "I don't see any signs of rainstorms anywhere," he said.

"Give it another hour or two," she replied. She backed out of the parking space. "Look to the southwest, that's usually where they come from. I just hope we've given Edward Bentz enough time to get from wherever he's been to Betty Fields's place. I'm eager to see why he was visiting my mother."

"I'm eager to ask him a lot of questions," Jackson replied. He hoped there was a reasonable explanation for Edward Bentz's sudden move to Mystic Lake. He hoped they'd discover that the man had family here, that he'd grown up here and decided it was the place he wanted to retire.

Otherwise Jackson would have to consider if he was a potential link between the crime that had occurred in Bachelor Moon and what had happened here in Mystic Lake.

By the time Maggie pulled up in Betty Fields's driveway behind a white panel van, Jackson's head was spinning. A high dose of adrenaline pulsed through him at the sight of the van, which hadn't been in the driveway when they'd been here before.

If somebody was going to kidnap two people, they would need transportation, and a panel van was the perfect vehicle for such an undertaking.

Betty answered Jackson's knock. She was a petite older woman with a head of snowy-white hair and the smile of a gentle soul. "Come in and get out of the heat," she exclaimed. She ushered them into a small, cool formal living room with a sofa, two chairs and a polished coffee table.

The scent of pot roast rode the air, and Jackson's stomach rumbled despite the fact that they'd had a late lunch.

"I know you're here to speak to Edward. He's just gone to his room until dinnertime. I'll call him and you all can talk in here." She gestured them to the sofa and then disappeared down a hallway.

The sound of a knock on the door, a murmur of voices, and then she returned with a tall, broad-shouldered man following at her heels. "I'll just be in the kitchen if you need anything," she said, and quickly scurried from the room.

Edward Bentz was a handsome man with sandy hair and hazel eyes. He gave them both a pleasant yet curious smile. "You wanted to speak to me?" he asked.

Jackson did the introductions, noting the slight dilation of Edward's pupils as he realized they were FBI agents. "What have I done to warrant the interest of the FBI?" He sank down in the chair opposite the sofa.

"The first thing is that you visited my mother before you left town," Maggie said.

"Your mother?" His brow wrinkled and then

smoothed out. "Of course, you're Katherine's daughter. I should have recognized the resemblance."

"What was your business with her?" Maggie asked, her tone more aggressive than usual.

"Business? No business. I knew Bob Stevenson. I used to deliver medical supplies all over the southern portion of the States. I met Bob and we became friendly and then a year went by when I didn't see him. I saw him again about three months ago and he mentioned that he'd married and divorced a woman from Mystic Lake. I got the impression he'd done her wrong, and so when I came to town I decided to look her up. She's a lovely lady, by the way."

Jackson could tell Maggie wasn't sure if she believed him or not. "I understand you're from my neck of the woods," Jackson said. "Baton Rouge?"

Edward grinned. "I'd know that accent anywhere. I called Baton Rouge home for a long time, although my roots are here in the Midwest."

"Ever hear of a place called Bachelor Moon?" Jackson asked.

Edward frowned again. "No, I don't believe I know the place. Is it near Baton Rouge?"

"Not far from there," Jackson replied. "So, why does a man move from Baton Rouge to Mystic Lake?"

"I came into a little money, an inheritance, and decided my traveling-salesman days were over. I was sick of the big city and remembered passing through here once when I came to a conference in Kansas City. I wanted a small town, and this seemed to be the perfect place."

Although he spoke earnestly and his facial features showed no signs of lying, as he'd talked his body had shifted slightly away from Jackson, and his feet pointed toward the door.

When Jackson began to question him about his whereabouts on specific dates, Edward got downright shady, not remembering where he'd been or who he'd spoken to, professing that since he'd been making trips back and forth to Baton Rouge he wasn't sure what days he was where.

He couldn't provide receipts for gas or travel, didn't have records of what motels he'd stopped at on his trips. "I didn't know any of this would be important," he exclaimed. "I'm just a retired salesman looking for a quiet life. Why would I want to hurt a sheriff and his wife?"

Why indeed?

By the time they left Edward, Jackson was more confused than ever. There was something about the man he didn't trust, but he couldn't make the pieces fit. According to Bentz, he'd never even met Cole Caldwell.

Dammit, they needed a break, he thought as he slammed out of the house when they were finished with the interview. He got into the car and noted the dark clouds gathering in the sky.

Maggie had been right. It looked as though a storm was brewing, and he felt it simmering inside him. The frustration that roared through him was the same that he'd felt when he'd been working the case in Bachelor Moon, only bigger and stronger.

He couldn't imagine working back-to-back cases that yielded no answers, no closure. He was used to solving crimes, not allowing crimes to beat him, and at the moment he felt totally beaten.

Maggie slid into the car and turned to look at him. "Food," she said. "I sense a raging beast not only in the sky but also in the seat next to me. I can't do anything about the coming storm, but we need to feed the beast before he fully emerges. We'll stop at the diner before we leave town."

He looked at her in surprise, wondering when in the time they'd spent together she'd come to know him so well.

"I just feel like we can't get a damned break," Jackson said when they were seated in the Mystic Lake diner, where they had eaten lunch earlier in the day.

They'd already ordered burgers and fries, but even the promise of imminent food didn't relax the tense lines on Jackson's face.

"You'll feel better after you've eaten," she said. She took a sip of her water as outside the window where they sat, the sound of thunder rumbled, and lightning flashed in the distance. Hopefully they could eat quickly enough to get back to her place in Kansas City before the rain came.

"What did you think about Bentz's story?" he asked.

She released a tired sigh. "To be honest, I don't know what to think. I definitely believe we need to dig a little deeper into his background, confirm his previous employment and whatever we can find out through legal channels. We don't have enough on him to get any kind of a warrant to dig too deep."

"I did a cursory background search on him already. He has no criminal record. The man has never even gotten a speeding ticket," Jackson said with obvious disgust.

"Maybe it is just a coincidence that he showed up in town around the same time Cole and Amberly went missing. Maybe he really is exactly what he says he is, a traveling salesman from the South who decided to retire to a small Midwestern town." She sighed once again. "And maybe the moon is really made of green cheese."

"So, you didn't believe him," Jackson replied. He paused as the waitress arrived with their orders.

"I don't know what to believe anymore," she admitted. "I feel like my brain has been taken out, scrambled and shaken and then set back in place. Maybe I'm just exhausted. I haven't been sleeping very well."

"That makes two of us," Jackson replied.

She had a feeling he wasn't sleeping well for the same reason she wasn't. Each night that he'd been beneath her roof, she'd tossed and turned, trying not to think about him in the next room, trying not to play and replay the kiss they'd shared. The energy between them snapped and crackled, and fighting it had become exhausting.

He picked up a fry from his plate without enthusiasm and glanced out the window where the storm clouds had created a false sense of twilight.

It was the first time since she'd met him that he appeared discouraged, without a smart quip or that twinkle in his eyes. His unusual demeanor made her even more afraid for Cole and Amberly.

"You aren't giving up, are you, Jackson?" She voiced her concern.

He smiled and shook his head. "No way. I'm a persistent man when I'm going after something I want, and I want answers. No, I'm not giving up, but I am discouraged by our lack of progress."

He picked up another French fry, but it was obvious that food wasn't going to solve the problem of his frustration. He took a bite of his burger and then shoved his plate away with a deep sigh.

"Actually, I thought I was hungry, but I guess I'm not," he admitted.

She raised a brow. "Take note of this moment… Jackson Revannaugh isn't hungry." She looked down at her plate and then back at him. "To tell the truth, I'm not really hungry, either."

He gazed toward the window where it appeared darker than it had moments before. "Maybe we should just get out of here and try to beat the storm to Kansas City."

"Sounds like a plan to me," she agreed. "We can always eat later at home, since you stocked my pantry and fridge with enough food to feed a small army for a month."

Thunder crashed overhead as they left the diner, followed by a sizzle of lightning that slashed through the dark sky. Thankfully the rain hadn't begun, although it threatened to fall at any minute.

Marjorie had just pulled out of the diner and started down Main Street when she noticed in her rearview mirror that a motorcycle was following too close for her comfort.

"Crazy drivers," she muttered under her breath. At that moment her rearview mirror on the outside of her door exploded. She screamed at the same time Jackson flew into action. He unbuckled his seat belt, pulled his gun and turned to look out the back window.

"He's got a gun. Don't let him pull up next to us. Keep him behind us." Jackson rolled down his window and leaned out as Marjorie fought down panic.

The back window exploded inward and Marjorie stifled another scream while Jackson cursed and fired back. "Get us off this main road," he said. "Make a turn and try to lose him."

Marjorie didn't know the town of Mystic Lake well, but she stepped on the gas and then took the next right turn at a speed that had them nearly riding on two wheels. She quickly made another turn to the left, but could hear the whine of the motorcycle still behind them.

Jackson popped off a couple more shots, but in her rearview mirror Marjorie saw the motorcyclist zig and zag in erratic movements to dodge Jackson's assault.

As he made a move to pull up next to the side of the car, she turned the wheel and rode along the curb to thwart his actions, grateful that they were on a residential street with no oncoming traffic. Numb with fear, she turned left, then right and then left once again, lost in the maze of quiet neighborhood streets while the cyclist remained behind them.

She realized that as long as she was driving fast and taking corners at breakneck speed, he had no opportunity to shoot but instead had to focus on his own driving.

The fear dissipated when she focused on the simple act of survival. Training kicked in and a cold wash of determination swept over her. As Jackson fired again, the motorcycle fell back.

Marjorie didn't slow her speed or her evasive driving. She continued to race down streets. Disoriented as to place, she was stunned to find herself back on the road that led to Kansas City. A glance in her mirror showed her nothing, and an edge of relief coursed through her. It lasted only seconds, since the motorcycle roared into view once again.

"Just don't let him get next to us," Jackson said, his voice half lost from the wind blowing in the open back window. He was leaning so far out the passenger window she feared if she veered too sharply he'd fall out.

Once again the motorcycle roared forward, heading for the other lane of traffic. Marjorie jerked her wheel to keep him from coming up alongside the car.

She knew that if he got next to them he'd have a perfect shot to kill either her or Jackson, and she wasn't about to let that happen. If he was going to kill them, she was going to make him work for it.

As she saw the approaching lights from a car, she swerved back into her lane, and the motorcycle fell back. She was aware of her own breaths coming in small gasps, but she focused on keeping the car on the road.

If they could just make Kansas City there would be enough traffic that it would be much easier to lose their pursuer. She knew the city well, knew the best streets to take to throw him off.

Just get to Kansas City. It became a mantra in her head as her gaze shot from the mirror to the road. Raindrops began to splash on her window, and she had to turn on her wiper blades in order to see the road ahead.

She had no idea what Jackson was doing, only that he'd lowered himself back in the passenger seat but was still turned to face the back, where he could shoot out the busted window.

Her fingers were so tight around the steering wheel they cramped in pain, but she didn't dare relax her hold. She didn't even have time to wonder who was chasing them. All she could think of was getting to familiar territory where it would be more difficult for the man chasing them.

The rain came down harder, making visibility more difficult as the skies grew darker. She didn't want to turn on her lights, didn't want to make them a well-lit moving target.

Ten more miles and they'd reach the city limits. Ten more miles and she was certain they would find safety. If nothing else, she could drive right into the parking lot at the FBI field office, where she was certain a murderous motorcyclist wouldn't follow.

Seven miles, she thought. Six miles. She was eating up the highway at a reckless speed, despite the rain and the darkness.

Almost there. Surely she could get them to safety. The front windshield exploded outward and instantly another bullet found one of the tires. With a scream she twisted the wheel, bumping them over the edge of the highway and down an embankment, where the car rolled to its side.

Stunned, she remained buckled in place as she heard the whine of the motorcycle coming closer... closer.

"You okay?" Jackson's voice came from someplace next to her.

"I...I think so."

"We've got to get out of here."

The car lay on the driver's side, and she unbuckled her seat belt as Jackson climbed out the window. She fumbled around and found her purse, grabbed it and then allowed him to pull her up and through the window, as well.

The motorcycle appeared on the lip of the highway and went silent. "Run," Jackson whispered, and pointed in the distance to a stand of trees.

He grabbed her hand and together they ran like the wind, rain pelting them as danger got off the motorcycle. Apparently the lack of good visibility worked in their favor. They made it to the trees at the same time a tall, well-built figure started down the embankment toward their wrecked car.

Jackson squeezed her hand. "We can't stay in the area. Which way is the city?"

Marjorie paused a moment to get her bearings and then pointed. They took off running, aware that within minutes the motorcycle man would realize they weren't in the car and would come after them.

Chapter Nine

Jackson had no idea how long they ran. It felt like forever. At any moment he half anticipated a bullet to the back, but as they got farther and farther away from the car, some of the fear that had lodged in the back of his throat began to wane, the rich, comfortable and familiar emotion of anger taking its place.

He'd heard no sound of the motorcycle that might indicate they'd been followed. They finally landed in an alleyway between a pizza joint and a tattoo parlor, where they leaned against the brick wall of the restaurant and drew in deep, gulping breaths.

The rain had stopped for the moment, although both of them were soaking wet. Wet was better than dead, he told himself as he waited for the stitch in his side to go away.

"I can't believe I wrecked the car," she finally gasped.

"You didn't wreck the car—a man with a gun wrecked the car. You drove like a professional race-car driver until he blew out that tire."

She gave him a grateful smile. Her blouse was wet and torn at one shoulder; the bottom of her slacks were covered with muck. Her hair hung in a bedraggled fashion, slicked to her scalp, and yet she looked beautiful.

He'd admired her as a gorgeous woman, but a new admiration for her as an FBI agent filled him. "We need to get someplace dry and safe," he said.

"I'll call for a car to pick us up." She started to open her purse.

"No, don't do that," he said quickly. She paused, and in the darkness of the alley, her eyes glittered like those of a jungle animal. "Right now I'm not in the mood to trust anyone but ourselves."

"You think that guy might be able to track us?"

"I don't know, but I'm not taking any chances. First the motel room and now this—things have definitely taken an unexpected turn. Do you have any idea where we are?"

"I know we're someplace downtown, but I'm not sure exactly where."

"You wait here. I'm going to go into the pizza place and get an address and use their phone to call for a cab." Her eyes lit with a touch of fear. "Don't worry," he assured her. "I'll only be gone a minute or two." She drew her gun and nodded. "Just don't shoot me when I come back," he said dryly.

The pizza joint was empty except for a young man with bad acne behind the counter. "Help you?" he asked in a tone of voice that indicated he'd prefer not to have to help anyone.

"I need this address and a phone to call a cab."

The kid rattled off the address and then picked up the receiver of a cordless phone on the counter and handed it to Jackson. "Cab numbers are taped to the wall by the front door. Our usual clientele like their beer more than their pizza."

Jackson walked over to the door and dialed the first number that connected him with a cab company. Assured that a cab would be there within the next fifteen minutes, Jackson hung up. He handed the kid behind the counter the phone and a ten-dollar bill.

"Hey, thanks."

Jackson didn't reply. He left and returned to the alley, where Maggie was huddled against the back. "Cab will be here in fifteen minutes or so."

"I can't wait to get home and get out of these wet clothes," she said as she put her gun back into its holster.

"We aren't going home."

She moved closer to where he stood at the mouth of the alley. "Then where are we going?"

"A hotel, and I don't want anyone on earth to know where we are for the night—not your boss, not mine and none of the law enforcement in Mystic Lake or here. Just you and me, darlin', for tonight we disappear off the face of the earth until we can fully process what just happened."

"I'm not sure I'll ever be able to process what just happened."

He heard the faint tremble in her voice. The adrenaline that had kept her functioning was apparently beginning to wear off. He wrapped an arm around her shoulders and pulled her close against him, their clothes slapping together wetly.

"I guess we should be grateful it was just rain and not hail or a tornado," she said, leaning into him.

"We should also be grateful that the shooter managed not to wound either of us."

He hugged her closer while they silently awaited the arrival of the cab. Although the night air was warm, she shivered against him and he mentally cursed the fact that they'd once again been caught off guard.

Whoever had been on that motorcycle had to have been watching them, waiting to follow them onto the highway, where he could hopefully kill them by either shooting them or causing a wreck that would render them helpless.

This was the second murder attempt they'd survived. He had to admit that he was a bit superstitious. How many lives did they have? Would the third time be a charm for the assailant?

There was no question in his mind now that the threat came from somebody in Mystic Lake. But who? They had spoken to dozens of people that day as they'd meandered the streets and stopped into stores.

It had begun to rain again, a soft patter that, at this point, couldn't make them any wetter. Nor did the rain distract from Jackson's thoughts.

Two things he knew for sure—the person who had chased them had been on a street-legal motorcycle, and he was left-handed. Jackson pulled out his cell phone and called the sheriff's office in Mystic Lake.

"Deputy Black," he said to whoever answered the phone. "Tell him it's Agent Revannaugh."

A moment later Roger Black's deep voice filled the line. "What's up?" he asked.

"First thing in the morning I want you to have ready for me a list of everyone in Mystic Lake who owns a motorcycle," Jackson said.

"Okay, want to tell me what this is all about?" Roger asked.

"We'll talk in the morning when we come in to get that list." Jackson disconnected and slipped his cell phone back into his pocket.

At that moment a cab pulled to the curb, and he and Maggie slid into the backseat. The driver was a bear of a man, with a full head of fuzzy red hair and a nose that looked as if it had been broken more than once. "Where to?"

"What's the best hotel in the city?" Jackson asked, and felt Maggie's surprised gaze on him.

"Best as in most expensive?" the cabbie asked. "Definitely the Woodbridge Hotel on the Plaza."

"Then that's where we want to go," Jackson said, and then leaned back in the seat.

Maggie leaned toward him, her eyes worried. "Jackson, that place is really expensive, and I'm not sure the agency will cover that kind of accommodations."

"Don't you worry," he assured her. "I've got this."

"Are you sure?"

"Positive. Just sit back and enjoy the ride. It won't take long and we'll be someplace safe and dry."

She leaned back against the seat and closed her eyes, and Jackson studied her in the light of street lamps they passed.

Once again her face was unnaturally pale, and even though her hands were clasped in her lap, he couldn't help but notice their slight tremble.

Adrenaline still pumped through him, wild and intense. He knew it would go away eventually, but not until he and Maggie were safely ensconced in a place where nobody would find them for the night.

He checked his watch, surprised that it was only just after eight. The chase had seemed to last forever, their run for safety even longer, but the entire thing from start to finish had lasted only about forty minutes.

He plucked at his wet shirt, looking forward to a shower and then a big towel to dry himself off. His mind clicked and whirred with his plans for the night.

By the time the cabbie pulled around the circular drive in front of the high-rise, high-dollar hotel, he'd made his plans and felt good about their safety for the night.

They got out of the cab, and Jackson paid the driver, who then zoomed off to head toward a staging place to await the next call.

The hotel lobby was tastefully opulent, gold and black being the main color scheme. Jackson led Maggie to an area near the concierge's desk. "Wait here," he instructed. "It should just take me a short time to arrange things for the night."

He strode toward the front desk, aware that both of them looked like something the cat had dragged in.

"Good evening, sir." The man behind the reservation counter didn't blink an eye. "How can I be of service to you tonight?"

Jackson told him exactly what he wanted, and within minutes the room had been paid for and he held two keys in his hands. "There are also several other things we'll need." As Jackson explained, the man behind the counter pulled out a pad and took notes.

"We'll be glad to accommodate you with everything you need," he said.

Jackson thanked the man and then went back to Maggie. "We're all set."

"I still can't believe you came here," she said as they walked toward the elevator bank. "A no-tell motel would have been just as safe as long as nobody knew where we were."

"My taste for motels has changed since somebody tried to kill us in one," he replied.

They stepped into the awaiting elevator, where Jackson used a key in a slot. "Trust me, nobody will think to look for us where we're going."

The doors whooshed closed and he watched Maggie's eyes as the elevator reached the top level of buttons and continued upward.

When the door finally opened it was on the quiet top floor. There were only three rooms here, and he led her to the door on the far left and used a card to open it.

"Welcome to your home for the night."

She stepped into the lush two-bedroom suite with a living room that boasted a white stone fireplace, a red plush sofa, two chairs and, to the side, a dining room table that would seat twelve.

She turned back to face him, her eyes gleaming and a smile of disbelief curving her lips. "Are you serious?"

He laughed. "As serious as a heartbeat. Tonight we live in luxury. I'd say we've earned it after barely escaping with our lives."

Her smile fell and her body began to tremble. He wasn't sure if it was because she was wet and the air-conditioning was cool or if it was the aftermath of trauma. He suspected the latter.

He pulled her into his arms and she pressed against him, as if seeking any heat that might remain in his body. He held her for several long moments and then released her.

"Go on, go check out your suite. There should be a jetted tub in there, complete with complimentary bubble bath. While you're indulging in that, I'm going to shower and order up some food. I'm suddenly starving."

She laughed, the first carefree burst of laughter he'd ever heard from her. "Why am I not surprised? I'll meet you back here after I'm clean and dry."

She practically skipped to her suite and he heard her excited gasps. She returned to the doorway, her eyes opened wide. "There's even a television in the bathroom," she exclaimed.

"Turn it on and watch something," he replied, delighted by her excitement.

"I'm going to get spoiled and then I'm probably going to have to order cable television when I get home." She flashed him a quick smile and then disappeared back into the suite once again.

Jackson turned and headed for his own room, a sinking feeling in his heart. Not only did he have to figure out who had tried to kill them not once, but twice, he also had to admit to himself that he was more than a little bit in love with Maggie Clinton.

MARJORIE LOWERED HERSELF deeper into the hot pear-scented bubble bath and released a deep, cleansing sigh. Awaiting her was not just a big fluffy towel, but also a pristine white robe that would serve as her clothing until bedtime.

She'd hung her blouse and slacks over the top of

the shower stall, hoping they would be dry enough by morning to put on again.

She frowned and sank lower in the oversize tub. The last thing she'd want to do in the morning was pull on the torn blouse and nasty, dirty slacks, but at least for tonight she'd be clean and comfortable in the provisions offered by the hotel.

The television was turned on to an all-news channel, the volume just loud enough to be heard above the bubbling jets that gently pummeled her body in pleasurable waves.

Never had she been in a place like this, and she wondered how on earth Jackson had managed to afford it. She used her toe to turn the knobs that would add more water, and then grabbed one of the complimentary bottles of shampoo and lathered up her hair.

She turned so that she could use the faucet water to rinse the shampoo and then reluctantly turned off the water, shut off the jets and pulled the plug. If she stayed in any longer she feared she might grow a tail.

The big towel was heavenly, soft and fluffy and enfolding her entire body. She moved from the tub to the enormous marble vanity complete with two sinks and a mirror that showed her tangle of hair and the paleness that still clung to her skin, making the handful of freckles on her face stand out more than usual.

As she finger combed her hair, she tried to keep her thoughts off the events of the night. At the moment she was warm and comfortable, but she knew if she allowed her mind to drift back in time, a new chill would not only sweep through her, but take complete possession of her.

One minute at a time, she told her reflection in the

mirror. Soon enough she knew that she and Jackson would be discussing what had happened. But for right now, she just wanted to indulge herself.

She found a small bottle of complimentary lotion that smelled of the fresh, slightly spicy pear bubble bath, and she rubbed it liberally over her shoulders and down her arms and legs.

She thought about using the hair dryer, but heard a knock on the front door and froze. Her purse with her gun was on the king-size bed in the bedroom.

She relaxed as she heard Jackson answer, the murmur of voices and the sound of a tray being delivered. She'd been so long in the bath apparently Jackson had already showered and ordered them a meal, which had just arrived.

It took her only minutes to discard the towel and reach for the robe that easily wrapped around her. She belted it and then eyed her reflection in the mirror one last time.

Twice they'd eluded death, but at least for tonight they would be safe. She left her suite and returned to the living room, where the table had been set for two. The plates were covered with metal containers hiding the visual sight of the food but unable to hold in the amazing scent that emanated from the plates.

Jackson wore a robe like hers and he looked hot as hell with his dark hair still damp and slightly messy and the material stretching across his broad shoulders.

"Just in time," he said as he caught sight of her. He smiled and pulled out one of the chairs at the table for her.

"Something smells delicious." She slid into the chair

and he removed the metal cover to reveal a beautiful steak, mashed potatoes and perfectly grilled asparagus.

"I wasn't sure what you'd want," he said as he took the seat next to her. "I figured this meal hits most of the food groups—meat for protein, potato for starch and veggies just because I figured you'd want some."

A basket of hot rolls and slabs of butter were also on the table, along with tall glasses of water. He'd poured her a glass of red wine, assumingly from the bar, and he had a glass of what she knew was bourbon in front of him.

He raised the bourbon glass and motioned for her to pick up her wineglass. "To us, for surviving." They clinked glasses, and then she took a sip of the wine. It warmed her from her mouth to her stomach.

"I say we eat and don't talk about anything too grim until we're finished with our meal," he suggested.

"Sounds perfect to me," she replied. She cut into her steak and took a bite. "I feel like I've died and gone to heaven."

"Not heaven." He grinned. "Just the Woodbridge Hotel."

They ate in silence for a few minutes, and then Marjorie looked at him in speculation. "Are you wealthy?"

"I suppose in some social circles I'd be concerned wealthy," he replied.

"Family money?"

"God, no." He laughed, as if finding the very thought amusing. "More like lucky money."

"What does that mean?" She cut a piece of asparagus and tried to tell herself she really wasn't that interested in his life, she was only making dinner conversation.

"I left home when I was sixteen. I continued to go to school, and after school I worked whatever jobs I could find. I slept in bus stations, showered in truck stops and did everything I needed to survive." He set his fork down and stared just over her shoulder, as if lost in the maze of his past.

"I managed to get through college on scholarships and still working whatever jobs I could find. When I graduated I had a little nest egg put away and I invested it in a company one of my roommates was starting up, a computer security company.

"By the time I joined the police force the company was widely successful and my buyout gave me more cash than I knew what to do with. Since that time I've invested smart and been lucky with those investments."

"So, if you're so rich, what are you doing working for the FBI? Why work at all?"

"The job is in my blood." His eyes flickered the dark blue that made her want to plumb their depths. "I can't imagine doing anything else."

She nodded, understanding exactly what he meant. She couldn't imagine anything else she'd rather be doing than working this job. She liked taking bad guys off the streets and making sure they were locked up where they belonged.

"I especially like the profiling aspect of the job, although I seem to be failing miserably at the moment," he added.

"The very best profiler wouldn't have enough information to work well in these circumstances," she replied. "And we said no talking about work while we ate."

"Right," he said easily, and took another sip of his bourbon. "I will say this, though—this is the first time I've felt completely relaxed, completely safe, since the night of the motel shooting."

She raised a brow. "You didn't feel safe at my house?"

"To be perfectly honest, I wondered when the bad guy or guys would figure out where you lived and attack us there."

She sucked in her breath at the very thought of the sanctity of her little home being compromised.

As they finished the meal, rain pattered against the windows and an occasional rumble of thunder was heard, but it was obvious the storm was passing and would soon be gone.

Once they had eaten they moved to the sofa. He sat first and patted the space right next to him. As she sat next to him he wrapped an arm around her shoulder.

"It's been one hell of a night," he said softly. "Was the car your personal vehicle?"

She nodded, trying to ignore the fresh scent of soap and male that emanated from him. "But I'm not worried about it. I have good insurance."

As she thought of the car...the bullets and how lucky they had been...a new chill took form in the depths of her, a chill that forced a shivering she couldn't control.

"Hey." He pulled her closer against his side. "It's over for now and we're still here."

Unexpected tears burned at her eyes and as they fell down her cheeks she swiped at them with an embarrassed laugh. "I don't know what's wrong with me. I suddenly feel like an emotional mess."

He tightened his arms around her. "You're crashing, darlin', and it's okay to do it right here in my arms." His voice was a soft caress that only made her tears flow faster.

Instead of attempting to suck them up, mentally realizing she couldn't do anything to stanch them, she turned so that her face was in the front of his robe and she sobbed into the fresh scent as he held her tight and caressed her back.

He didn't say a word and she was grateful for his silence. All she needed were his strong arms around her and the safety of his nearness.

When the tears had finally stopped, she sat up and swiped her face. "Sorry, I didn't mean for that to happen." Her gaze searched his. "I was just so scared," she admitted painfully.

He smiled and gently reached out to tuck a strand of her hair behind her ear. "I'll tell you a little secret—I was positively terrified."

Her eyes widened in astonishment. "But you seemed so cool."

"Inside I was quaking like a young man meeting his girlfriend's parents for the first time." Once again he reached out, this time to place the palm of his hand on her cheek. "Fear is good, Maggie. Fear is what keeps us alive. If you had no fear, then I wouldn't want you as my partner. You'd be dangerous not only to yourself but to me, as well."

She curled against him once again and released a deep sigh.

They were safe for tonight, but what happened tomorrow? Were they at risk staying in her home? They certainly couldn't stay here indefinitely.

Tomorrow new arrangements would have to be made, but she wasn't sure where they could go to escape the danger that felt as if it moved closer and closer.

Chapter Ten

Jackson didn't want to move. With Marjorie snuggled against him on the sofa, finally relaxed enough that she was no longer crying or shaking, he was reluctant to break the embrace.

But he knew they had to talk about the case, to discuss what had happened tonight and what it might mean. Hopefully tomorrow Roger Black would have a list of everyone in and around the Mystic Lake area who owned a motorcycle, and with that list he and Maggie could potentially figure out who had chased them through the rain with the intent to murder them.

She must have sensed that his thoughts were going in darker directions, for she sat up and wrapped her arms around herself, as if preparing for the discussion they had to have.

"It's obvious that the guilty party lives in or around Mystic Lake," he said.

She nodded. "I agree. Unfortunately we talked to dozens of people today, so it's impossible to single out any one person we might have spooked."

He frowned. "You know what bothers me about all of this? We aren't the only FBI agents asking questions. We aren't the only law enforcement people investigating. So why target us specifically?"

Her frown mirrored his. "What are you thinking? That these attacks are somehow personal and not about the case at all?" She shook her head. "You aren't even from around here, and I can say with confidence that there's nobody who cares enough about me to kill me."

Nobody cares enough about me.... The simple, stark words once again touched Jackson's heart despite his desire to the contrary. He raked a hand through his hair and tried to remain focused on the real topic of conversation.

"I don't know, maybe it's just a crazy thought. But Black has deputies walking the streets, and nobody has tried to kill them. Don't you have an agent working with you…Agent Forest?"

She nodded. "Adam Forest. But he hasn't been in touch with me about any threats or near-death experiences. Should I call him and double-check?"

"Not tonight and not from here. I don't want either of us using the phones here, or our cell phones for the night. Call me paranoid, but I don't know the enemy well enough to know what his resources might be."

"That's a scary thought," she replied.

"Better safe than sorry. We get to just talk to each other until it's time to go to bed." He looked at his watch. It was already after ten, but he didn't feel the least bit sleepy.

What he felt like was taking Maggie into his suite, stripping the oversize fluffy bathrobe off her body and making love to her, but he knew it was not only a natural reaction to stress, but also a bad idea all around.

Still, the spicy pear scent of her, the softness of her

hair and the memories of her sweet curves pressed tightly against his own, stirred that primal desire that Natalie Redwing had spoken of so eloquently.

"I just think you're wrong in believing this is anything personal," she said. "We have been the face of the investigation since it began. If our perp is from Mystic Lake, then the law enforcement there might be his friends or relatives, while we are strangers and easily disposed of."

He grinned. "Not so easy, after all. We're cats with nine lives."

"I'm not willing to trust our luck a third time. We need to figure this out, Jackson." Her eyes were so emerald and so earnest.

"We aren't going to figure it out tonight," he replied. "I arranged for a late checkout tomorrow so we have until noon to get out of here. I suggest we both sleep as late as possible and prepare for whatever surprises come next," he suggested.

"And there will be surprises, won't there?"

"Probably," he replied honestly.

"Should we plan on going back to my house or figure something else out instead?" she asked with obvious worry.

Once again Jackson released a deep sigh. "To be honest, I don't know the answer to that. It worries me that somebody found us in my motel room and then again on the road in your car."

"But nobody would be able to get my address from anyone at headquarters, and I'm not listed in the phone book. My neighbors don't know me well and certainly don't know what I do for a living." A wrinkle creased her brow. "I still think we'd be safe at my place as long as we don't unintentionally lead anyone there."

"I'm not willing to take that chance," he replied. "An internet search would cough up your address in an instant to somebody who was digging around for it. I think we need to go off the grid altogether," he said. "I'm thinking a motel somewhere and we don't tell anyone where we are."

"What about a car?" she asked.

"Do you trust Agent Forest?"

"With my life," she replied without hesitation.

"Then when we're ready to leave here tomorrow, call him and tell him to get us a rental under one of his friends' names, nothing that can be tied back to you or me. I'll make sure the fees are paid for in cash and we'll do as much work as we can out of your house. Let Roger Black and his men handle things in Mystic Lake under our advisement, but we stay away from that place until we have some better leads on who is willing to kill us."

He got up from the sofa and went to the well-stocked bar, where he poured himself another shot of bourbon. "Let's face it, darlin', at the moment we're just too hot, too visible to be seen in Mystic Lake. It's time to lie low and see what shakes out."

She unfolded her legs from beneath her. "I know you're right, but it makes me mad. I want to be out there. I want to have the pleasure of handcuffing the person who shot up my car."

"How about you go to bed and dream about it," he said. "You look tired, and it's been a very long day."

"What are you going to do?" she asked as she stood

and tugged her robe belt more firmly around her slender waist.

He picked up his glass of bourbon. "I'm going to finish this and then I'm going to hit the hay."

She smiled at him. "Those beds don't look like hay. They look big and luxurious and have pillow tops and cloudlike comforters."

She sighed and he took great delight in her obvious pleasure. "Then I'll just say good-night, Jackson."

"Good night, Maggie. Sleep well and we'll figure things out in the morning."

She disappeared into her suite and closed the door behind her. Jackson walked back to the sofa with his glass of booze and sank back down amid the accommodating cushions.

The bourbon was good, smooth and spreading warmth through him, but his thoughts remained dark. He couldn't shake the feeling that there was something more going on here than the investigation of the case of Cole and Amberly. But damned if he could figure it out.

Maybe it was actually a better idea to go back to Maggie's house rather than hide out somewhere. If the perp was as good as Jackson suspected he was, then eventually he'd figure out where Maggie lived, and some sort of attack would happen there.

They could be bait. They could be prepared and instead of chasing after their tails just wait for the bad guy to come to them. It was risky and he had to make sure Maggie was on board, but it made more sense than any other plan that had entered his mind since they'd arrived at the hotel.

First thing in the morning he'd contact somebody

to set up a security system at her place. *Fool me once, shame on you. Fool me twice, shame on me.* Twice they'd had close calls, and if they intended to stay at her place, then he wasn't going to make any careless mistakes.

They would be ready for the attack when it happened, and once they knew who was behind it they'd maybe get the answers they sought as to what had happened to the missing couple.

He finished his bourbon and carried the glass to the sink, then headed for his bedroom. He'd declined turndown service. He didn't want a maid coming in and disturbing their conversation by leaving a chocolate on the pillow and turning down the sheets.

His gun and holster were already on his nightstand and he took off his robe and slid naked into the bed. The mattress was heavenly, with just enough support to be comfortable.

He turned off the bedside lamp, and the only illumination was the faint moonlight that spilled in through the window, an indication that the storm had moved out of the area.

Closing his eyes, he tried to empty his mind, but flashes of the evening shot off like a kaleidoscope of pictures and scents and feelings.

He loved that Maggie had been so excited about the room, but he also knew she was a woman who didn't need this kind of opulence. She liked simple things, but he had a driving need to give her more.

It was crazy—she obviously didn't need anyone to take care of her, and yet he wanted to. He wanted to make sure her fridge held more than protein bars. He wanted her to have scented bubble bath and cable television.

He'd never felt like this before and he wasn't at all sure if he liked it. What he needed to do was solve this case as quickly as possible and hightail it back to his real life.

He smelled her before he saw her, that sweet pear scent that instantly aroused him. She stood in the doorway of his room. "Maggie?" he said softly.

"I'm looking for a nice Southern gentleman named Jackson," she said, her voice slightly husky.

"That would be me," he replied, his chest suddenly tight with anticipation.

"I thought you might be interested in a night of un-complicated sex with a woman who isn't looking for anything more than this night and this night only."

"Maggie…" He said her name in hesitation. God, he wanted her. He thought he might even need her. But he knew things she didn't know, things that would forever stand between them and make any future impossible.

He didn't want her to pretend that she could be a one-night kind of woman if at heart she wasn't.

"It would only be a one-night deal," he finally managed to say.

"I wouldn't have it any other way," she replied. Before he could respond she shrugged out of the robe, leaving her gloriously naked in the moonlight.

Chapter Eleven

There was not a fiber in Marjorie's being that felt any hesitation as she approached the side of Jackson's bed. She knew that probably part of what had driven her to his room was the fact that they'd both nearly died, that she was probably suffering some innate need to connect and affirm life.

But there was also a huge dose of desire that had been burning inside her soul for him that she'd finally decided to give in to. The primal energy that Natalie Redwing had spoken of had exploded, and she wanted to burn in those flames.

When she reached the side of the bed, he threw back his covers to invite her in. She didn't hesitate. Even though she knew he wasn't a man for her lifetime, he was the man she wanted for this night.

She slid between the sheets and instantly he drew her against him. His naked body was hot and hard against hers as their lips met.

The kiss was wild, desire untamed and unleashed. Their tongues lashed against each other. He tasted of command and possession and bourbon, and she couldn't get enough of his mouth.

At the same time their hands moved frantically,

caressing naked flesh in exploratory strokes. She loved the way his broad back felt beneath her fingers, the muscles that moved and bunched beneath the palms of her hands.

His hands played down her back, as well, forcing a shiver of pleasure to sweep through her as he used first light and feathery touches and then harder, more determined ones, sliding down to the base of her spine.

Their kisses continued until finally he slid his mouth down her jawline and she gasped for air, feeling as if he had stolen all that there was in the room with his intimate nearness.

His body was hard and she liked the way her soft curves fit against him. She'd expected complete mastery, a sense of utter possession. What she hadn't expected was the tenderness.

His lips moved down her throat, lingering as if he loved the taste of her skin. "My sweet Maggie," he murmured. "I've wanted you since the moment you picked me up at the airport."

"And I think I've wanted you even before I met you," she replied, knowing it didn't make sense. But she'd been hungry for a man like him, a man who would challenge her, a man who, with his sexy smile and twinkling eyes, could weaken her knees and make her want him to take her to bed.

She gasped again as his mouth possessed one of her nipples, his tongue swirling around the hardened tip and creating a river of sensation that shot straight to her center.

Tangling her hands in his hair, she was aware of his complete arousal, that he was physically ready to take her at any moment. But he seemed to be in no hurry, his mouth attending to one breast and then the other. This raised her desire for him inside her to an unrelenting ache of want.

She moved her hands to his smooth chest, loving the heat and hardness of his taut muscles. He lay half on top of her, giving himself room to maneuver his hands and lips to explore her body.

His mouth left her breasts and trailed a blaze of fire down the flat of her stomach. She attempted to lie still but couldn't, and instead shivered from the sheer pleasure he evoked.

Reaching a hand down between them she grasped his hardness and he raised his head to gaze at her, his eyes glittering with raw emotion in the nearly dark room.

With their gazes still locked, he caressed a hand down to touch her between her legs. A moan escaped her as she raised her hips to meet him.

She was a firecracker ready to fire, and he was the detonator that would make her explode. He moved his fingers a little faster against her sensitive skin.

She moaned again, this time louder. Heat flooded through her, and every nerve ending in her body tingled with imminent release. And then she was there, exploding into a million pieces and shooting out to space.

Before she returned to earth, Jackson positioned himself between her thighs and entered her. This time he moaned as he buried himself deep within her.

He hovered just above her, holding the bulk of his weight on arms that trembled. Taut neck muscles let her know he fought for control as he moved his hips to thrust him slowly in and out of her moist heat.

He paused a moment, looking down at her, and he smiled that sexy grin that shot straight to her heart. "I feel like I'm finally home, Maggie."

She raised her legs to wrap around his back, drawing him in deeper and also trapping him against her. "For tonight you are home," she replied softly.

Her words seemed to galvanize him back into action. He stroked in and out of her with a quickened pace, and a new release built up inside her. He was all that mattered at the moment, the taste of his mouth, the feel of his hands on her skin, her hands on his. She was ravenous and he fed her hunger.

Tears sprang to her eyes as waves of pleasure threatened to drown her, and at the same time he stiffened against her, climaxing with a groan of her name.

She'd expected him to roll over and out of the bed. He'd gotten what he'd wanted, was finished with her. But instead he rolled to the side of her, leaned up on one elbow and gently stroked a strand of her hair away from her cheek.

Maybe he was just waiting for her to get up and leave his bed, his room, she thought. She started to sit up, but he pushed her back down.

"Don't be in such a hurry," he said with that lazy grin stretching his lips. "After-sex conversation is almost as important as presex talk. You were amazing."

"I never knew it could be like this," she said as she relaxed back into the sheets. "I mean, I never before… uh… It's never been so intense for me before."

He looked at her in surprise. "You mean you've never had an orgasm before?"

Her cheeks warmed and she was grateful for the

darkness that hid the blush. "My previous partner was more interested in his own pleasure than mine."

"Then he definitely wasn't a gentleman," Jackson replied. "In fact, I believe that makes him an ass."

She laughed. "He was kind of an ass. In fact, he was worse than that—he was a boring ass."

He reached out and stroked his hand against her cheek. "You're too much woman for that kind of a man."

"You mean I need somebody who aggravates me, who has a ridiculous Southern charm and is totally hot to look at?" she teased.

"And that would be me," he agreed.

"You do realize you're quite arrogant."

"Not arrogant," he protested. "I'm just good and I know it. I'm confident."

"And I'm sleepy now. I think it's time for me to use the bathroom and say good-night." She slid out of the bed, not self-conscious in her nakedness after what they'd just shared.

"Use my bathroom and then come back to my bed." He sat up, the sheet falling down to expose his beautiful chest. "I'd like to wake up in the morning with you in my arms."

She hesitated. There was nothing more she wanted at the moment than to crawl back into his bed and wake up with him next to her in the bed. But her desire for it scared her. He wasn't supposed to mean that much to her. This was just supposed to be a sex thing, not a warm and fuzzy continuance until morning.

Desire won over good sense. She went into his bathroom and when she returned to the bedroom he lifted the sheets to once again welcome her into his bed.

The minute she was beneath the sheets, he pulled her into his arms, spooning her as if they'd been lovers for years. She hated to admit to herself how much she liked the feel of his body against hers, his arm possessively around her waist and the soft warmth of his breath against the back of her neck.

She didn't want to admit that he had managed to crack the shell that had encased her heart since the time of her father's death, that he'd made her not just like him, but love him more than a little bit.

It was a feeling she didn't want to have, a feeling she knew would only lead to heartbreak. She knew her partner and she knew his life was far away from her life in Kansas City, not just in miles but in emotional distance.

She knew their case was in bad shape. They'd been nearly killed twice and yet she felt as if the clearest, most present danger she faced at the moment was the luxury of loving Jackson.

It was just after seven when Jackson awakened, Maggie a warm pillow he'd wrapped in his arms as he slept. Although he knew they had a hundred things to accomplish today, he was reluctant to leave the bed.

He'd suspected there was a wealth of passion hidden deep inside her and last night she'd released it all, giving to him the gift of her vulnerability and her fiery need.

It was funny that she'd been the one to remind him that it was a one-time deal. That was all he'd ever wanted from the women in his life, but he found himself dissatisfied and wanting more from Maggie.

But, of course, he knew that more wasn't possible. If he ever bared his soul to her, she'd run for the hills.

The sins of the father would come back to haunt him, and he'd rather walk away from here without her ever knowing where he came from and the choices he'd ultimately made that should have been made long before.

With these thoughts in mind, he silently slid from the bed and padded into the living room where several boxes had been delivered at some point during the morning.

He opened one of them to find underwear, a pair of jeans and a polo shirt all in his size. He carried the items into Maggie's suite, where he showered and dressed without awakening her.

Once showered and dressed, he called room service for coffee, deciding to wait for Maggie to wake up to order breakfast. He hoped she slept late. He had no idea what time they'd eventually gone to sleep, but he knew it had been the wee hours of the morning.

He stood in front of the expanse of windows in the living room and stared outside, trying to keep his mind off Maggie and instead focused on the work that had to be accomplished that day.

If they went through with his plan to return to Maggie's house, then the first thing he had to do was arrange for a state-of-the art security system. He wanted outside monitors so they could see who might approach the house from any direction. He wanted to arrange for extra firepower besides their two handguns.

Last night's attack had led him to believe that somehow things were coming to a head. The assailant had taken a million chances in chasing and shooting at them on the open highway. Witnesses might have seen him, somebody might have recognized his motorcycle. Somebody was getting desperate to quiet him and Maggie.

But surely whoever was behind the murder attempts could reason that even if he killed the two of them, more FBI agents would take their place.

That meant either their perp wasn't that bright or something deeper was at work. Either scenario worried him, and this morning he was filled once again with the frustration of the entire case.

Two people missing now over two weeks, no clues, no bodies. What were they missing? The frustration was a familiar one, the same that he had felt while working the case in Bachelor Moon.

A soft knock on the door announced the arrival of coffee. He opened the door, handed the man dressed like a butler a twenty-dollar bill and took the tray from him.

He carried it to the table, noting in satisfaction that there were two cups and the silver coffee carafe was huge. He poured himself a cup and then returned to the windows where he stared unseeing outside.

Maybe he should stash Maggie someplace safe and use himself as bait. The instant the idea entered his head he knew he was thinking like a protective lover and not as a professional agent. Besides, there was no way she'd agree to such a plan. She would want to be involved as a trained FBI agent on the case, not tucked away like a delicate piece of china.

While he didn't regret a minute of the night before, it concerned him that making love to Maggie had only made him want more from her. He knew they were ill-fated lovers at best.

As if drawn from her sleep by his thoughts, she

appeared in the living room, clad in the hotel robe. "Ah, coffee," she said, beelining toward the table where the carafe and a cup awaited her.

"And a good morning to you, too," he replied with an amused smile.

She poured the coffee, took a sip and then flashed him a bright smile. "Now it's a great morning."

He gestured for her to sit at the table, and he joined her there. She took another sip of her coffee and quirked one of her eyebrows upward. "Where did you get the clothes?"

"It's amazing how accommodating the concierge at a hotel can be when persuaded with cash." He pointed toward the sofa. "That box has fresh clothes for you."

She sighed in obvious relief. "Thank goodness. I was really dreading having to pull on the stiff, torn, dirty clothes from last night." Her eyes gleamed as she held his gaze. "You better not have ordered up some red silk cocktail dress for me to wear out of here today."

He grinned. "It crossed my mind, but I figured why start the day on a bad note after such a great night."

She eyed him over the rim of her cup. "It was a great night if you forget the motorcycle maniac and the trek through the rain. So, what are the plans?"

"First up is breakfast." He moved a room service menu in front of her. "Personally, I'm going for the Woodbridge special—bacon, eggs and toast with pancakes on the side."

"I'll take the same without the pancakes," she replied. "I seem to have worked up an appetite overnight." Her eyes twinkled teasingly.

Jackson placed the order and then returned to the

table. "After we eat, and we're ready to check out, you can call Agent Forest and see if he can get us a car. I noticed out the window that there's an outdoor restaurant named Willie's, with a dedicated parking lot about a block away. Tell Agent Forest to leave the car there with the keys under the mat."

"Okay, and then what?"

"First thing we do is drive to Mystic Lake and get the list of motorcycle owners from Roger, and then how do you feel about heading back to your place and setting us up as bait?"

Her eyes narrowed. "I like it. You're banking on whoever is after us being able to find us at my house. And we'll be waiting for them."

"Exactly. I'll use some of my own resources and see to it that by the time we get back to your place, we'll have a security system in place." He stopped talking as a knock fell on the door. "That should be breakfast."

The food was delicious, the conversation not so much fun as they discussed the pitfalls and perils of their plan. "I'll make sure we have monitors to give us vision of all areas of your yard. If anyone approaches we'll see them before they get too close."

"The monitors will have to be watched 24/7," she replied. "We'll have to take shifts."

"We'll do whatever we need to do." He poured a liberal dose of syrup over his stack of pancakes and then cut into them. "We'll put everything in place, but what I'm really hoping is that once we see that list of motorcycle owners Roger has prepared, we'll have the name of our suspect, or at least more people to seriously look at."

"I'm glad we've decided to do this. I'd much rather

take chances and work the case than hide out somewhere and let others do our job for us," she said. "I want this solved, Jackson, and I want to be a part of the solution."

She got up from the table. "I'm going to shower and get dressed and then we'll get out of here and back to work. I might just like being a worm dangling on a hook waiting for a shark to bite."

He watched her as she grabbed the box from the sofa and then disappeared into her suite. He took a bite of his pancakes, but his appetite was gone.

Was this a mistake? Intentionally placing themselves in a spot where a killer might come to call? He didn't mind taking the risk himself, but the idea of anything bad happening to Maggie set his heart plummeting to the ground.

He just hoped that when or if the time he might need to save her came, he would be the agent he thought he was, the man he believed himself to be.

Chapter Twelve

Purple. He'd bought her a jewel-tone purple blouse and black jeans that hugged her legs as though they'd been tailor-made for her. In the box there had also been a lilac bra and silk panties.

He was incorrigible, she thought as she pulled on the clothes after having taken a long, hot shower. She'd thought she wouldn't like him. She'd believed that within two days his charming talk and easy ways would force her to strangle him. But instead, he'd captivated her.

Despite all her intentions to the contrary, she knew without doubt that Jackson Revannaugh was going to be her very first heartbreak, and she might as well prepare herself for it now.

Once she was dressed and they were ready to walk out the door, she made the call to Adam Forest to arrange for the car, and at the same time, Jackson spoke to somebody about the security system he wanted installed at her house. "We'll meet you at Maggie's in half an hour or so to let you inside," he said.

With plans made to begin their day, they left the luxury suite of rooms and headed out of the hotel. "By the way, you look gorgeous," he said as they walked side by side to the restaurant where they'd pick up the new car.

"Thanks. I've never had silk underwear before."

He shot her a glance that threatened to melt her into a puddle of goo. "Don't even talk about it—the image I get in my brain will force me to throw you down right here on the sidewalk and have my way with you," he teased.

"One-night wonder, that's what we were," she replied lightly, needing to remind not just him but herself that what they had shared the night before wouldn't happen again.

Once again the late-July sun beat down with unrelenting heat, although the air wasn't as humid as it had been the day before.

They walked briskly. With their plans made for the day, Marjorie just wanted to stay focused on the work and not on how hot Jackson looked in his tight black jeans and white polo shirt. He wore the shirt untucked, with his belt and gun making a slight bulge on his side.

She'd always felt safe in her home, but Jackson was right—if somebody wanted to find out where she lived all it took was an internet search. She'd worked enough cases that she was surprised she'd never considered how easily somebody could find her for some sort of retribution before.

She should have had a security system in her house a long time ago, but money was so tight and she'd never felt the need for one until now. And when this case was over, she'd figure out a way to keep the security system in place.

She'd made arrangements with Adam to leave a black rental car at the farthest end of the parking lot from the restaurant. She was surprised, when they spied the car, to see Adam sitting behind the wheel.

He got out of the car when he saw them approach. Adam was a handsome man, with slightly long blond hair and pale blue eyes that looked cold and distant.

Marjorie knew he was anything but that. He was definitely one of the good guys, a talented profiler who loved research and was brilliant with a computer.

"I thought you were just leaving the keys under the mat," she said as they reached the car.

He nodded a greeting to Jackson, and then looked at Marjorie. "I just wanted to make sure the two of you were okay. You both had your phones off last night."

"We had a little encounter with a Mad Max character who tried to kill us," Jackson explained. "We decided to take the night and lie low. Was there a reason you tried to call?"

"No, just a check-in." He held out the keys to the car. "It's rented in the name of Charles Bachman and paid up the next two weeks."

Jackson took the keys. "Thanks."

Adam looked at Marjorie once again. "Let me know how I can help."

"Actually there is something you can do. Check and see if John Merriweather knows anyone who might own a motorcycle. If you find out anything give me a call." Aware that Jackson apparently intended to drive, Marjorie slid into the passenger seat and waved at Adam, who stepped back from the car.

"He's crazy about you," Jackson said once they were in the car and headed to Mystic Lake.

Marjorie looked at him in surprise. "Don't be silly. We've worked together on several cases. He trusts me."

Jackson had almost sounded jealous, but surely she'd misinterpreted his tone.

"Adam is a talented agent who overcame a horrible childhood. He doesn't trust easily and he's, for the most part, a lone wolf. But enough about Adam."

"So, you've come around to my thinking that John Merriweather remains a solid suspect," he said as he pulled onto the road that would take them to Maggie's house.

"I'm keeping an open mind," she replied. "It occurred to me this morning that all John would have to do was sell a couple of his paintings under the table for cash and he'd have enough money to hire himself a hit man. There would be no way to follow the money and he could keep himself distant from the violence."

"Smart thinking, but if that's the case he hired a local yahoo instead of a professional hit man. If this was a professional, we'd probably both already be dead."

She couldn't help the small shiver that swept through her at his words. He glanced at her and caught her midshiver. "Are you sure you're up to this? I'd love to drop you off at some out-of-the-way motel and let me be the worm on the hook."

"We're partners, remember? There's no way I'm going to let you go all macho on me. Is this about what happened between us last night?"

He shot a quick glance at her. "Maybe a little," he admitted. "I have to confess that a little protective streak I didn't know I had has reared its head where you're concerned."

"I'm an agent first, Jackson, and then a woman."

He grinned. "Darlin', you were all woman last night."

Her cheeks warmed in a familiar blush. "But that was then and this is now. Whether you like it or not, I'm dangling on that hook right next to you."

"I figured that would be your answer." He pulled into Maggie's driveway, where a panel truck was already parked. "Sit tight," he said as he opened his driver door. "This should just take a minute."

She watched as he met with the tall bald man who got out of the truck. Interesting that there was no writing or graphics on the side of the truck to indicate that it was part of a home security business. Jackson handed the man a key she assumed was the copy of the one she'd given Jackson to her house.

"Everything should be done by the time we get home from Mystic Lake," he said when he was back behind the wheel. "I told him to go subtle but effective. I don't want the bad guys to know we have anything in place."

"Sounds like a plan."

They fell silent as he headed toward Mystic Lake. For no particular reason she felt as if they were approaching the end, that the list of motorcycle owners they got from Roger might hold their answer.

Their list of suspects was still rather pathetic, with Jeff Maynard, Jimmy Tanner, Edward Bentz and John Merriweather, but if one of those names appeared on Roger's list, then they could potentially have enough evidence to get all kinds of warrants to execute to gather even more personal information.

Even the FBI had red tape and rules that had to be followed, but Roger might hold the clue that would get them past the red tape.

Once the case was solved she saw no happiness for

anyone. Cole and Amberly were probably dead, which would scar little Max for years to come and leave behind many people to mourn.

Jackson would return home, taking with him a source of energy, of life that had filled the little house with his presence.

She had a better understanding of her mother now. It wasn't stupidity that had driven her mother into the arms of con men, it had been loneliness and the need to believe she was all the wonderful things they told her she was even as they fleeced her out of what money they could get.

As Marjorie thought of being held in Jackson's arms the night before, of the magic of their lovemaking, she realized that despite her fight against it, she had fallen for his smooth charm, his sexy smile and the bits and pieces of the man she'd seen beneath his facade.

The case would eventually be solved, and Jackson would go home, but she knew it would take her a very long time to get him out of her system, to not think about him and ache for what might have been.

DEPUTY ROGER BLACK was in his usual spot behind Sheriff Caldwell's desk. Next to the desk were wooden file cabinets, the tops stacked with files. A photo of Amberly and Cole sat on the desk, and Jackson knew that picture would be a constant reminder of his missing boss.

He stood as they entered his office. "I was just about to get some coffee. Would either of you like a cup?"

"No, thanks, we're good," Maggie replied.

Roger sat back down. "It took me half the night, but I got the information you requested." He shoved several documents aside and grabbed a sheet of paper and handed it to Jackson. "I included not just the street-licensed bikes, but also the names of folks I know who have dirt bikes."

"Thanks, I appreciate it." He took the list and folded it up in his pocket, making the decision that he and Maggie would pore over it when they got back to her place.

As the three of them caught up with the case as it stood, Jackson tried to ignore Maggie's presence. He should have never bought her those tight jeans and that purple blouse. The purple was a perfect color for her red-blond hair and intense green eyes.

Most of the time when he woke up after having sex with a woman, he was ready to bolt as quickly as possible. But Maggie was different. She was special, and each time he looked at her, a new desire returned to torment him.

They had to get a quick solve and he had to get away from her. She threatened the very lifestyle he'd chosen for himself. When he'd seen her with little Max, he'd immediately seen her with another dark-haired little boy—his child.

He'd never thought about having a family, having children, before in his life, but Maggie made him think about those things. And he couldn't go there, especially not with her.

He focused back on Roger's musings about the case. "I just don't understand any of it," he said. "Usually when something bad happens here in town, eventually we hear rumors that yield clues. But this time we've heard absolutely nothing. Even the drunks down at

Bledsoe's haven't given up any information that might be useful."

He reared back in the chair and shook his head. "Cole wasn't just my boss, he was my friend. He was a good man who most folks in town liked and respected. He had no dark secrets that might have come back to bite him. I knew him."

"You're speaking about him in the past tense," Maggie said.

Roger shrugged. "After all this time, it's my belief that they're dead. Nobody would keep them alive so long without a ransom note filled with some sorts of demands."

"And yet we don't have their bodies," Jackson said.

Roger frowned. "I figure at some point in the future some farmer will stumble on the bodies in the middle of a field or hidden in some woods."

"And you don't have any theories as to why the bodies wouldn't be just left out in the open for somebody to find?" Jackson asked.

Roger shook his head. "I'll be honest with you, we've been out of theories and ideas about this case since the very beginning. We were hoping the officials in Kansas City might come up with something."

"So far, we have nothing," Jackson said. "Except for somebody who has Maggie and me in their sites."

"And you don't know for sure where that threat is coming from?" Roger asked.

"I'm guessing somebody from here, but the first attack happened in Kansas City, and last night's attack came from somebody who was here in town and followed us. We're working the case from both ends," Jackson replied.

"And I'll keep working from this end. Hopefully that list I gave you will help." Roger stood, as if aware that their conversation had come to a natural end.

Minutes later they were back in the car and headed home. Jackson was grateful for Maggie's silence, as his head spun with suppositions and possibilities.

They had a meager list of potential suspects, and it was quite possible that the person responsible for Amberly and Cole's disappearance wasn't even on that short list.

It was possible that they hadn't even made personal contact with the perp, that he was flying far enough below their radar to be completely off the screen.

Every person on the list in his pocket would have to be fully investigated. Even though he had no real evidence, he still believed the person responsible for the crime, the person who had attempted to kill him and Maggie twice, was from Mystic Lake.

"Home, sweet home," he said as he pulled into Maggie's driveway. There was no sign of the panel van that had been there before.

Jackson cut the engine on the car and pulled his cell phone from his pocket. It took him only minutes to connect with the tech who had done the work on the house and learn the details of what had been done.

"Okay," he said as he dropped his cell phone back in his shirt pocket. "We're all set."

Together they got out of the car and as they approached the house he saw Maggie looking at the structure carefully, as if expecting to see trip lines and big cameras.

He laughed and she looked at him. "What? Were you expecting rolls of barbed wire and steel bars?"

She grinned sheepishly. "I was expecting something."

"The eyes that protect us are no bigger than a fly. We aren't hooked up to any monitoring system. I told him to put the camera monitors in your bedroom, and if anyone tries to breach the house through a door or a window, a siren will sound that should not just awaken us but the entire neighborhood."

"The wonders of modern technology," she replied as she unlocked the door. They stepped inside and he immediately moved to a keypad on the wall and punched in a series of numbers.

"The code is random. I'll write it down for you and you need to memorize it. Too many people make the mistake of making their codes their birthdates or part of their social security or some other sequence of numbers that a determined bad guy could ferret out."

Maggie nodded and headed down the hallway to her bedroom. Jackson tried to ignore the sway of her hips in the tight jeans as he followed behind her.

He hated to admit that he thought maybe he'd told the tech to set up the system in her bedroom just so that he could actually see the room where she slept. He had a feeling that this visit would be his first and his last to the room that belonged to her alone.

The bedroom was a shock. He'd expected monotones of black or gray and instead he walked into a flower garden. A floral spread covered the bed, with pink throw pillows in the center. A pink shaded lamp stood proudly on the nightstand, next to a creased paperback written by a famous profiler.

The dresser top held an array of lotions and perfumes and a picture of her and her mother. Above the dresser, the wall now held several medium-sized television screens that gave views of the front of the house, the back and both sides.

"We should be snug as two bugs in a rug in here," he said.

She turned and her lips turned up in knowing amusement. "You did this on purpose. You had him mount the monitors in here so that we'd have to spend time together in my bed if we wanted to see what was happening outside the house."

"You wound me to the core," he protested. "I just figured if you wanted to keep this system after I'm gone it would be easier for you if the monitors were in here."

She eyed him dubiously, and love for her buoyed up inside him, unwelcome and unwanted but there nevertheless. "Let's head to the table and take a look at this list that Roger gave us," he said gruffly.

He needed to be out of this room, where glimpses of her femininity showed, where her scent filled the air and made his desire to possess her again surge.

Once they were in the kitchen and seated across the small table from each other, he pulled out the list that Roger had prepared and scanned the names. Disappointment flared through him and he shoved the list in front of Maggie.

Her brow wrinkled as she read, and the wrinkle turned into a sigh of frustration. "None of our potential suspects are on it. That means we're going to have to investigate all these people, because it's possible the perp is one of these names.

"I'll fax the list to Adam and he can get on the investigation from the office," she said, her disappointment evident in her voice. "I'd so hoped that we'd have an answer by now, or at least a path to follow."

"Maybe Adam will be able to sort out who could be a potential threat on the list and who definitely isn't," Jackson said thoughtfully. "It would have been nice if Roger had given us not just names but ages, as well."

"It would have been nice if that motorcycle would have hydroplaned in the rain last night and crashed," she said dryly. "But nothing about this case has been nice so far."

"Last night was nice." He couldn't help himself. The words were out of his mouth before his brain was engaged.

She looked up at him, and her eyes held a soft vulnerability he'd never seen before. "You're right. It was nice, and the truth of the matter is I've allowed you to get deep into my heart, Jackson."

She raised a hand to halt his response, though he wasn't even sure what he intended to say. "It's my problem, not yours. You have no ownership in it other than you are who you are. Women find you irresistible, and I guess this just confirms that I'm a normal woman at my core."

"Maggie...I..."

Once again she stopped him from speaking, this time shoving back from the table and talking over him. "I didn't realize how empty my life was until you came along. When you leave here I will be making some changes."

She gave him a small smile, defusing some of the tension in the air. "First thing I intend to do is order cable television. The second thing is that I'm going to have a long, difficult talk with my mother and get her settled into someplace more affordable."

"I'm glad to hear that," he said, surprised to discover a lump in the back of his throat.

"I'm also going to stop eating so many protein bars and learn how to cook. I'll miss you desperately when you're gone, but eventually I'll get over you because I'll have to. You'll break my heart when you leave here, Jackson, but we both know we weren't meant to be anything but partners. And now I'm going to go check out the monitors."

She didn't wait for him to say anything, but scurried out of the kitchen and disappeared down the short hall. Jackson remained at the table, his heart twisting like a flag in a windstorm.

She loved him. That was basically what she'd just confessed. She loved him and he loved her. But he would leave her brokenhearted. What she didn't know was that she wasn't the only one who would have a broken heart when Jackson returned home to Baton Rouge.

Chapter Thirteen

Four days. It had been four long days since the security had been installed and she and Jackson had been cooped up together waiting for something to happen.

Four days since she'd foolishly confessed her feelings for Jackson, and since that time they had been stiffly polite to one another, unnaturally impersonal.

She hadn't intended to tell him how she felt about him, it had just happened, and now she wished she could take it back, return their relationship to the easy, slightly flirty and effective partnership they'd shared before.

Equally as difficult was the fact that nothing new about the case of Amberly and Cole's disappearance or the attacks on her and Jackson had come to light. They were dangling themselves out there like worms on a hook, but the shark hadn't even circled them yet.

They'd stopped throwing out theories and ideas to each other, having exhausted the topic to death. Jackson paced the small confines of the house like a caged animal, his frustration and pent-up energy nearly driving her mad.

They both needed something to happen. A blip on the monitors, the ring of an alarm would almost be a relief. At least it would break the tense monotony of waiting for something to occur.

She'd been in touch with her director several times during the past few days. She'd learned that the case in Bachelor Moon was still an open one, that the three people who had gone missing from the Bachelor Moon Bed and Breakfast had yet to be found.

Both the FBI in Kansas City and Baton Rouge were still reluctant to draw the conclusion that the two crimes were related, especially given the attacks that had happened on Marjorie and Jackson…a distinct difference from anything that had happened in Bachelor Moon.

It was early afternoon and Marjorie was seated at the table, staring unseeing out the window. She sat up as Jackson came into the room. "I feel like a shriveled-up worm left dangling on a hook that nobody wants to bite," she said.

"Trust me, I feel the same way." He threw himself into the chair opposite her and raked a hand through his hair. "I don't know, maybe this hole-up-and-wait idea was a bad one."

She shrugged. "It made sense to me at the time."

"Yeah, it made sense to me, too, but I didn't expect it to take so long for somebody to come after us."

"Maybe he's intentionally torturing us," Marjorie said. "Maybe he knows we're holed up here just waiting for an attack to happen and so he's decided to wait us out."

"Maybe," Jackson said absently. He stared out the window, obviously lost in thought.

Why did he have to be so handsome? Why couldn't they have sent her an overweight, belly-scratching, beer-burping agent to work as her partner? Why did it have to be Jackson?

He looked at her, his eyes a fathomless midnight blue that let her know his thoughts were deep and dark. "I can't help but believe that the case in Bachelor Moon and this case are related."

"But nobody else seems to want to make that connection, and then there's the difference of the attacks on us," she replied.

"The cases themselves are virtually identical. Missing people obviously taken unaware, no clues left behind, no ransom communication from the kidnapper… nothing varies from case to case except the two attacks on us." His frown deepened.

"So, you're back to believing that maybe the attacks weren't about the case, after all, but somebody who wants one or both of us dead for another reason." She leaned toward him, trying not to notice the familiar scent of him. "But neither of us can think of anyone who would want to hurt us."

"I know, I know," he exclaimed irritably and got up from the table to pace the small confines of the room. "I feel like I've lost all my instincts as an agent, like I'm floundering in a vast sea and not seeing the rock right in front of my boat."

Even though she knew it was the worst thing she could do, she got up from the table and walked over to where he'd finally stopped pacing and stood by the refrigerator.

His arms were folded across his chest, his eyes hollow as he stared at her. She placed a hand on one of his arms, wishing she could take away his frustration, wishing she had the answers that would take that hollowness out of his eyes.

What she really wanted to do was take him by the hand and lead him into her bedroom, fall into bed with him, where they could both escape the frustration and sense of time being stopped by losing themselves in each other.

But she knew that wouldn't help anything; it would only make matters worse. Instead she laid her hand on his arm and gazed deep within his eyes. "Jackson, we're doing what we think is right. Whether somebody is trying to kill us for personal reasons or because of the case, we're here, and eventually they'll get tired of waiting and will make a move. We just have to be patient."

He uncrossed his arms and she dropped her hand to her side. "Patience isn't something I consider a virtue," he said dryly. "In fact, I find it a real pain."

She smiled at him, grateful to hear a bit of humor in his voice. "Maybe we need to decide what we're going to cook for dinner," she suggested, hoping to lighten his mood even more.

"I'm not in the mood for food at the moment," he replied. He walked back over to the window. "Besides, we're out of milk." He turned suddenly. "Isn't there a convenience store at the corner?"

"Actually, it's two blocks away."

"I think I'll drive up and get a gallon of milk." His eyes were no longer hollow but instead held a glint she hadn't seen before.

"What are you up to?" she asked warily.

"Nothing. Just a fast trip to the store, that's all." He grabbed the car keys from the counter. "I'll be gone five minutes. You know the drill, keep the doors locked, the security system engaged and I'll be back before you know it." He set the keys back on the table. "On second thought I think a quick walk will do me good."

He didn't wait for her reply, but headed for the door, his footsteps heavy and determined. She followed behind him and locked the door, then engaged the security after he left.

Instantly she felt two things…an immediate loss of energy and life in his absence, and a bit of relief that his frantic energy was momentarily gone.

She walked back into her bedroom and watched on the monitor, spying him as he walked down the driveway and then disappeared from her sight.

Just watching him walk away from the house shot a tiny stab of pain through her heart…a precursor of what was to come when the case was solved and he went back to his home in Baton Rouge.

She left her bedroom and went back into the kitchen. Maybe she'd surprise him and she'd do the cooking for dinner tonight. She opened the freezer door and stared at the packaged meats, trying to make up her mind between pork chops and chicken breasts. She finally settled on the pork chops. She pulled them out of their packaging and placed them in a baking dish, and at that moment the doorbell rang.

She nearly jumped out of her cotton underwear at the sound. It was too soon for Jackson to be back already. She raced to her bedroom and looked at the monitor that viewed the front porch.

A man stood there, a man who looked like an older

version of Jackson. As he knocked, she raced from the living room to the front door.

"Who is it?" she called.

"My name is Jerrod Revannaugh. I'm looking for my son, Jackson, and was told that he was here." The voice was deep, smooth and Southern.

She hesitated a moment, fingers paused over the security keypad. There was no question in her mind that the man on her front stoop was Jackson's father. He not only sounded like his son, but looked like an older model of Jackson.

All she knew was that father and son had suffered some sort of falling-out years before, but surely Jerrod Revannaugh wouldn't be here if he didn't want to make some sort of connection with Jackson.

Decision made, she punched in the numbers that would disarm the security and then unlocked the door and opened it. In person, the resemblance between Jackson and his father was nearly breathtaking.

Surely she had nothing to worry about in letting him in to wait for Jackson. She had no idea what had caused the break between father and son, but it had to be a good thing that Jerrod was here.

"Mr. Revannaugh, I'm Marjorie Clinton," she said as she stepped aside to allow him into the small living room. "Jackson just went down the street for a minute and should be back anytime."

"Well, then, I'll just have to hurry a bit, won't I?" He gave her a charming smile and then stuck her in the side of the neck with a needle.

She yelped at the sting, and immediately the effects of whatever he'd given her took hold. Her legs turned to rubber and she reached out to grab him around the neck to keep herself from falling to the floor.

Without effort, he scooped her up in his arms. "It's okay, darlin', I'll take good care of you."

Her last conscious thought was that she hated Jackson's father...because he'd called her darlin', and the only man in the world she wanted calling her that was Jackson himself.

JACKSON WALKED BRISKLY, breathing in the air that smelled of fresh-cut grass and sunshine instead of the sweet floral scent of Maggie.

They were out of milk, but his walk had two goals. Retrieve the gallon of milk and make a phone call where he knew Maggie wouldn't be able to hear him.

Maybe he was being paranoid, but he couldn't shake the fact that the attacks they had survived had been somehow personal in nature. There was only one person in Jackson's life who might have a motive to kill him, and that was his father.

Last Jackson had heard, his father was behind bars at the state prison just outside Baton Rouge. Jackson knew he was there because he'd been one of the people who had been responsible for putting him away.

Jerrod Revannaugh had been a con man for all of Jackson's life. He could have easily been one of Maggie's stepfathers, a man who scammed women out of their life savings through fraud and deception and danced away unscathed...until the last time.

At sixteen years old, Jackson knew what his father was, and he'd walked away from him without a backward glance. Jackson had gotten on with his life and rarely thought about the man who'd raised him, a man who had attempted to instill the same lack of morals in his son.

They'd met again six years ago, when Jackson was contacted by law enforcement officers who were investigating the death of an elderly woman. Although it appeared to be a tragic slip and fall in a bathtub, the fact that her much younger husband had been married five times before to older women who'd found themselves nearly destitute after encountering the same man made them suspicious. The dead woman's husband was Jackson's father.

Jackson clenched his fists at his side as he reached the convenience store. Instead of going inside, he walked around to the side of the building, pulled out his cell phone and punched in a number he'd called several times over the past couple of years.

The murder charges hadn't stuck in the case against Jerrod Revannaugh, but a dozen counts of fraud by deception had, and he'd been sentenced to six years in prison.

When his call was answered, he asked to speak to the warden and then identified himself. "I'm calling to check on prisoner 22356," he said. The pause on the other end of the line tensed every muscle in Jackson's body. "What's up, Warden?" he asked when the pause went on too long for comfort.

"Somebody should have contacted you. Prisoner 22356 was released at six o'clock this morning."

Jackson nearly dropped his phone. Jerrod was out of prison, and he definitely had a reason to hold a grudge against Jackson, who was a prosecution character witness in the trial.

He hung up and slipped his phone back into his

pocket and then went into the store and bought the milk. As he walked back to Maggie's his head whirled.

Jerrod was Jackson's dirty secret, a secret he hadn't shared with Maggie because of her past with her mother and men like Jerrod. He was afraid of being judged, afraid that she would somehow believe the apple hadn't fallen far from the tree.

Jerrod was a threat to him, but if Jerrod had been released from prison in Baton Rouge early that morning, there was no way he could be behind the shooting at the motel or the chase by the shooting motorcyclist.

Unless he had an accomplice. Unless he had somebody on the outside who would be willing to do his bidding for part of the fortune Jackson guessed his father had hidden in some offshore account.

As he thought of all the people they had spoken to, all the people who had been potential suspects, the name Edward Bentz exploded in his forehead. He was a man who had traveled back and forth from Kansas City to Baton Rouge over the past couple of weeks... in the time that Jackson had been here working on the case.

Was it possible Edward had been behind the attacks? He'd certainly been vague about where he'd been during to two incidents. They should have dug deeper, they should have looked harder at him.

Suddenly he couldn't get home fast enough. Knowing that his father was out of jail put a whole new spin on things, and he needed to come clean to Maggie.

If there was anything that would put a halt to any feelings she might have for him, surely it would be the fact that he came from the same kind of men who had scammed her mother out of her fortune.

Still, it was information she needed to know, because Jackson had a feeling he'd realized the answer behind the attacks on them…his father wanted him dead, and Maggie would have just been collateral damage.

He started to unlock the front door, but realized it was already unlocked. Had Maggie forgotten to lock it when he'd left? Damn, he needed to remind her that locks and security systems didn't work if they weren't used.

"Maggie?" he called as he walked toward the kitchen. She wasn't in the living room or in the kitchen. He put the milk in the refrigerator, noted the pork chops in the baking dish and then went in search of her, assuming she was probably back in her bedroom.

"Maggie," he called again. This time when there was no response, his heart began an irregular rhythm of anxiety. Her house wasn't big enough for her not to hear him.

He paused at the bathroom long enough to check that she wasn't in there and then headed on to her room. Empty. His heartbeat accelerated.

He knew there was a door in the kitchen that she'd told him led down to a basement she used for storage. He raced back to the kitchen, flung open the door and thundered down the stairs into a small basement that held nothing but a couple of boxes labeled Winter Clothes.

Gone.

She was gone.

There was no way she would have left the house alone. She knew the dangers of being outside without having him along as backup.

He raced back up the stairs and went to the video equipment in her bedroom. He knew the security tapes were looped and he could replay them to see if anyone had come to the door.

His hands trembled as he punched the buttons to rewind the tape and he gasped in shock as he saw his father on the front porch. "Don't open the door. Please, Maggie, don't open the door." He whispered the words desperately even as he saw the front door open.

He froze, watching the monitor and moments later his father walked out of the house, carrying an obviously unconscious Maggie in his arms.

Instinctively he grabbed his gun, wishing he could shoot his father's image and make him drop Maggie. He wanted her safe, away from the man Jackson knew was a sociopath.

The monitor didn't show Jerrod getting into a car—he simply walked out of sight with Maggie in his arms. Jackson remained immobile, unsure what his next move should be, as terror threatened to burst his heart right out of his chest.

He knew he should be doing something, searching for her, but he didn't even know where to begin. Edward Bentz...Mystic Lake.

Edward Bentz had to have the answers. There was no doubt in Jackson's mind that the mild-mannered traveling salesman had been his father's minion. Jackson had to get to Mystic Lake. Hopefully, Jerrod would keep Maggie alive as a bargaining chip, for Jackson knew what his father wanted most was to kill Jackson.

Within minutes he was in the car and driving faster than he'd ever driven in his life toward the small town. If Bentz wasn't in his rented room, then Jackson would head straight to Roger Black and see to it that every law enforcement official in Mystic Lake was looking for Bentz and the newly released prisoner who had Maggie with him.

Dammit, he should have realized what was going on the minute it entered his mind that the attacks on them might be personal. But he'd been certain his father was still locked up and he hadn't thought of Jerrod being devious enough to hunt Jackson clear across the country to a case he was working.

He hadn't tried anything like this in all the years he'd been behind bars. Why now? *Why not now?* he countered. Who knew what drove Jerrod Revannaugh besides naive, lonely, wealthy women?

Maggie. His heart cried her name and the love he'd never felt for any woman before filled his soul. Maggie. She had to be all right. He had to find her and make sure she survived this horror he'd brought to her doorstep.

Chapter Fourteen.

Maggie came to and with a dazed semiawareness realized she was bound at her ankles and wrists, and tape covered her mouth, making it impossible for her to scream for help.

Dark… She was in the dark in a small space that smelled of oil and gasoline, and through her groggy hangover she realized she was in the trunk of a moving vehicle.

As the full implication of her predicament exploded in her brain, panic fluttered her heart and surged bitterness up the back of her throat.

She swallowed against it, knowing that panic would accomplish nothing. She remained still, lying on her side, and took several deep breaths in and out through her nose.

Think, Maggie, don't panic, she told herself. Thankfully her hands were bound in front of her with what felt like duct tape. She knew the futility of trying to slip or rip the tape away. She assumed her ankles were bound in the same way. She tested the strength of the tape, attempting to pull her ankles apart, but there was no give at all.

He must have been watching the house, she thought.

When he saw Jackson leave, he took the opportunity to engage her. She'd been a naive fool, thinking that maybe he was there for some sort of happy reunion with his son.

She should never have opened the door to him. But she had, and now she was in the back of the trunk of a car carrying her to an unknown destination for some unknown purpose.

Her heart raced faster. One thing was clear. Jerrod Revannaugh didn't intend for her to walk away alive from whatever he'd planned. Not only had he kidnapped an FBI agent, but he'd introduced himself to her, allowed her to see his face.

She was already a dead woman.

The minute she'd opened her front door, she'd signed her own death certificate. The only thing she didn't know, that she couldn't understand, was why this had happened.

Why her? She'd never met Jackson's father before, knew virtually nothing about him. So why had he taken her instead of just waiting and dealing with Jackson?

Somehow she knew she was a pawn between father and son. Jerrod probably believed that Jackson loved her, that she would be a useful tool to get his son to do something. What he didn't know was that Jackson didn't love her. And now she understood why he was probably incapable of loving somebody too deeply. Who knew what kind of childhood he'd had with a man who could drug and kidnap a woman?

She shoved away thoughts of Jackson, thoughts that caused pain as her love for him remained undiminished by the current events.

She had to figure out a way to get out. She'd read somewhere of a case of a woman who'd been imprisoned in the trunk of a car and she'd managed to punch out a back taillight and get another driver's attention.

Disoriented in the darkness, the first thing she did was scoot around the small space, trying to get her bearings. She was sideways in the trunk and she tried to position herself so that her fingers could search for a trunk release inside.

She didn't even think about what she might do if she did manage to pop the trunk. At the very least she could potentially sit up and maybe get somebody's attention. Worst-case scenario was that they were traveling in an area where there were no other people around, and her actions would only enrage Jerrod Revannaugh.

Deciding anything was better than just lying there waiting for whatever he had planned, she wiggled and squirmed until her fingers had traced every place she thought a release would be and found nothing.

Unwilling to be defeated, she located one of the back taillights and began to use her bound feet to bang against it. Again and again she slammed her feet into the back of the taillight, until she had to stop to catch her breath, a difficult thing to do with her mouth taped closed.

Sweat ran down the sides of her face, and the T-shirt she'd put on that morning stuck to her. The temperature in the trunk had to be nearly a hundred degrees. If Jerrod kept her in here too long she'd die of the heat and dehydration.

She made several more kicks at the taillight and

then gave up, unwilling to expend the energy for what appeared to be a futile attempt.

Where was he taking her? She had no idea how long she'd been unconscious and so had no idea how long she'd been in the trunk.

Was he behind Amberly and Cole's disappearance? She frowned. No, that didn't make sense. He couldn't have done something to them to bring Jackson to Mystic Lake. There was no way he could have guaranteed that Jackson would be sent here from Baton Rouge. Unless he was a company man...unless he'd had a hand in appointing Jackson to his current assignment.

Her heart began to hammer once again as the car turned onto a gravel road, the rocks pinging beneath her. The car went over a short distance and then stopped. The engine went silent and Maggie could hear the sound of her own heartbeat filling the trunk. It was the sound of terror.

Every muscle in her body tensed as the trunk opened. She blinked against the sunshine that momentarily blinded her. Jerrod was nothing more than a tall, well-built silhouette as he leaned forward.

"We can make this easy, or you can make it hard," he said. "I'll pick you up and carry you, but if you fight me, I'll fight back, and with you trussed up like you are, it wouldn't really be a fair fight."

She nodded to let him know she understood. She would be a fool to fight right now. She'd have to wait and see if an opportunity presented itself later...if she had a later.

He leaned down and picked her up as if she weighed no more than a child. As she got her first vision of where they were, her heart sank.

In the middle of nowhere, that was where they were. She didn't even see any landmarks that she recognized. Ahead of them was a large shed with a tractor stored inside and a smaller shed to the side that was probably used for a variety of equipment.

He carried her to the smaller shed and as they drew closer she saw that it was solid and well built on a slab of concrete. He laid her on the ground and then unlocked the padlock on the door.

Once again sheer, unadulterated terror filled her. She tried to roll away, even knowing in her head that it was nothing but the pathetic move of a desperate woman.

He turned back to her and laughed. "Where you going, darlin'?"

She wanted to scream at him to stop calling her that. There was only one man in the world who had the right to call her darlin', and at the moment she feared for his life as well as her own.

Once again Jerrod picked her up and carried her into the dark confines of the shed. It was completely empty and the concrete floor was hard against her body.

He left her there but returned only moments later, this time with a flashlight and a couple bottles of water. He set them on the floor just inside the door.

"You can scream your head off out here and nobody will ever hear you," he said, and to her surprise he pulled out a knife and sawed through the tape on her feet.

He motioned toward her hands and she quickly held them out. She watched him cautiously as he removed the tape from her wrists and then ripped off the piece that had been across her mouth.

She thought about rushing him, but she was too weak and he had not only the knife in his hand, but she suspected he also had a gun somewhere on his person.

"Why?" The word croaked out of her dry throat as she managed to raise herself to sit on her butt. "Why are you doing this?"

"Why?" He laughed, although there was no warmth in his cold blue eyes or in the tone of his mirth. "I raised that boy and taught him everything I knew and he turned his back on me, became a damned FBI agent. Six years ago I got myself into a little legal problem and my son, my own flesh and blood, testified against me. I wound up being sentenced to six years in jail. He betrayed me, and the price for that is his death."

"What did you do with Amberly and Cole?" she asked, her mind reeling with all the information she'd just learned.

"Who?" His handsome face twisted into a confused frown as he stared at her.

"The sheriff of Mystic Lake and his wife."

"I don't know anything about them. All of my energy, all of my resources have been used to keep tabs on my dear son. You two have had the luck of the Irish so far. The men I've hired have been unusually inept in completing a simple death or two. But I'm here now, and to be honest, this is the way it should be. I should be here when it's time for Jackson to pay. I've had six years to stew and plot, to enjoy the vision of his death."

For the first time as he spoke of killing his own son, his eyes lit with life, and Marjorie recognized that she was looking into the eyes of pure evil.

"I'm leaving you with a flashlight and some water. I'm not inclined right now to kill you, but I do take great joy in the fact that for the next couple of hours my son will have no idea where you've gone or if you're dead or alive."

"Jackson won't care. He's nothing more than my partner," she protested.

"Oh, he cares, and once I contact him he'll come for you. Your white knight riding to your rescue, but unfortunately, the white knight won't survive to see another morning."

"Wait!" she cried as he stepped out of the shed.

As a reply he slammed the door closed and she heard the sound of the padlock being clicked into place and once again she was plunged into utter darkness and despair.

JACKSON REACHED BETTY FIELDS'S house in record time, a new fear crashing through him as he saw that Bentz's panel van wasn't in the driveway.

Of course it wasn't, he thought. Because Jackson was relatively certain that the panel van had carried Maggie away. He had no idea where his father might be holed up with Maggie, but he knew in order to get some answers he had to find Edward Bentz.

A knock on the door was answered by Betty. "Agent Revannaugh, how nice to see you again." She smiled sweetly.

"Where's Edward?" he asked, politeness gone beneath urgency.

"Well, I'm sure I don't know. He left earlier but didn't mention where he was going." Betty's forehead wrinkled. "Is there a problem?"

"Call the sheriff's office if he shows up here," Jackson said, his feet already moving him back to his car.

Panic simmered in his veins, a panic he refused to allow to blossom into its full potential. Panic didn't allow rational thought, and he had to think.

With Edward gone, his next stop was at the sheriff's office. He was led into the office where Roger Black sat behind the large desk. Roger must have sensed something, for he stood, his brow wrinkled. "What's happened?"

"Maggie is gone."

Roger's frown deepened. "Gone? What do you mean she's gone?"

"She's been kidnapped by my father. I saw it on the security video at her house."

"Why would your father want to kidnap your partner?" Roger asked as he sank back down in the leather chair behind the desk.

"Look, I don't have time to give you all the reasons why. We don't have the luxury of chatting about my father or my past with him. All you need to know is that he took Maggie and I believe Edward Bentz is involved."

"Bentz?"

Jackson wanted to reach across the desk and slap Roger upside the head. "I need you to get off your ass and get your men out looking for Bentz's van. I want him found sooner rather than later."

"No need to get all riled up." Roger stood once again and walked around the desk to stand before Jackson. "Just take a breath, man, and tell me what else you need from us."

Jackson sucked in air, trying to calm the nerves

that had his body on fire. "My father's name is Jerrod Revannaugh. He was released this morning from
a prison in Baton Rouge. I believe he's now either in
Kansas City or here in Mystic Lake."

His chest tightened and he clenched and unclenched
his hands into fists at his sides. "I'm guessing he's
here because I believe he hired Edward Bentz to keep
track of me."

"What does he want from you?" Roger asked.

"He wants to kill me, but at the moment I'm more
afraid for Maggie's life than mine."

"Have you got a picture of your father?" Roger
asked.

"No." Jackson sighed impatiently. There was too
much talk and not enough action going on. "You can
get a photo of him off the internet, but right now you
need your men to be looking for Bentz's van. My gut
says if we find Bentz, we'll find my father and Maggie."

"Excuse me a minute and I'll get the process
started." He walked around Jackson and disappeared
from the room. Jackson assumed he was going to talk
to his dispatcher and get the word out to all units working the streets.

Something had to happen fast. He knew his father,
he knew the black soul Jerrod possessed. With every
minute that passed, Maggie's life was in danger.

As he waited impatiently for Roger's return, his
gaze darted around the office, thinking idly that all
the clues to everything that had happened in the town
might be here.

Hopefully one of Roger's men would see Edward's

van seconds after the call went out. If Jackson didn't get to Maggie, if he couldn't save her, then he'd be worth nothing.

Shame and humiliation had already made him keep the secret of who his father was, what kinds of crimes he'd committed. Now his shame and humiliation might be the very cause of Maggie's death.

"No," he whispered, his knees nearly buckling at the thought of losing her. Rage and fear forced his eyes closed for a moment as visions of Maggie filled his head.

Her childlike excitement in the hotel suite, the laughter that was a rare and beautiful gift and the unbridled passion of her lovemaking all combined to create his love for her, a love that was too deep to explain.

He opened his eyes and his gaze instantly fell on the top of the wooden file cabinets. He frowned as he saw something there he hadn't noticed before.

A pair of black gloves.

A pair of black motorcycle gloves.

He took a step around the desk and saw a gray helmet half-hidden next to the wastebasket. His blood ran cold. Roger hadn't been on the list he'd given them of motorcycle owners. Why would he leave himself off?

He moved back to where he'd been standing when Roger left the room. As the deputy returned, Jackson stopped him before he could get all the way into the room.

"You own a motorcycle, Deputy Black?"

Roger's face paled. "Yeah." He gave a forced laugh. "Guess I didn't put myself on that list I gave to you.

I didn't even think about it. I keep it in storage most of the time."

"What's that?" Deputy Morsi joined the conversation.

"I just learned that Roger here owns a motorcycle," Jackson said, his voice deceptively pleasant.

"Yeah, he rides it most days, but hasn't ridden it for the last week or so," Morsi replied.

Something snapped inside Jackson. The motorcycle chase…the near-death drama. Roger's guilt-ridden expression. With a roar of rage unleashed, Jackson attacked Black, tackling him to the floor as his hands wrapped around the big man's neck.

"Hey…hey," Deputy Morsi exclaimed in panic as he drew his gun, obviously unsure who he should point it at, his fellow deputy or an FBI agent.

"You're part of it," Jackson growled out as his hands pressed tighter against Roger's neck. "You were the one who tried to kill us."

"I don't know what you're talking about." Roger had to work to get the words out as his face reddened from a lack of oxygen.

"I'll kill you right now if you don't start talking," Jackson said.

Roger's face grew even more red as his fingers scrabbled to loosen Jackson's hold on his throat. Realizing he couldn't break the contact, he hissed out an okay.

Jackson released his hold and as he got up he pulled Roger's gun from his holster and held it pointed to the lawman's chest. "You'd better start talking or I'm going to start shooting."

Jackson ignored Fred Morsi and several other deputies who had gathered behind him in the hallway. "Where's Maggie?"

"I don't know." Roger remained on his butt on the floor, rubbing his raw throat.

Jackson took a step toward him and placed the barrel of the gun against his forehead. "Jeez, I swear I don't know. I was hired by your father to get rid of you. I never wanted to be sheriff. All I wanted to do was retire, and he offered me enough money to make it worth my while. You're right, I was the one who chased you on the motorcycle, and I was in contact with Bentz, who was hired to keep track of your movements, but I swear I don't know where Jerrod has Agent Clinton. I swear to God I don't know."

Jackson took a step backward and handed Roger's gun to Deputy Morsi. "Arrest this man for attempted murder. We'll figure out more charges as we wind up this case."

He left the office as Morsi was locking handcuffs on his coworker. He stomped back to his car, got inside and realized he had no idea where to go.

His head dropped to the steering wheel, and hot tears burned at his eyes. Maggie. His darlin', Maggie. Where was she? Was she already dead? He hated his father, but he hated himself even more for not being man enough to tell Maggie the truth about the man who had raised him, a man capable of killing not just his own son, but the woman his son loved.

Chapter Fifteen

The dim shine of the flashlight did nothing to penetrate the dark corners of the shed. Maggie sat in the very center, having exhausted every means of escape she could think of.

She'd tried to break down the door, had checked every area of the walls and the flooring to see if there was a weakness she could exploit, but there was nothing.

Tonight she would die.

She'd come to a final resignation about it, although a million regrets came with her acceptance of her fate. She wished she would have laughed more and worried less. She wished she would have taken more chances, reached out for more happiness.

She should have told her mother that all their money was gone and it was time for Katherine to live within her means. Marjorie wished she'd enjoyed her time on earth a little bit more. Dammit, if nothing else she should have allowed herself to get cable television.

A giggle bubbled to her lips. She knew it was a hysterical reaction to her circumstances. She was laughing to keep from weeping. She wanted to weep for Jackson. Even though she knew they hadn't been meant to be together, she could cry for what he'd given her. He'd opened her up to trusting. He'd made her realize she could love a man deeply.

She wished she'd had a chance to tell him she loved him one more time, but if even given the chance she wouldn't do it. She belonged in Kansas City, and he would go back to his home in Baton Rouge. She'd known there wasn't a future with him, but surely as she waited to die she could pretend.

Having already drunk one bottle of water, she was reluctant to open the second bottle that Jerrod had left for her. She had no idea how long she'd been inside the shed or how much longer she might be captive here.

She knew instinctively that this shed would not be her coffin and the only tiny modicum of hope she had left was that somehow when Jerrod came to get her out of here, she could escape.

What hurt the most was the certainty that she would be used to give Jackson as much pain as possible. Jerrod would twist Jackson's feelings for her, no matter what they were, into something ugly, something that would haunt Jackson if he lived or would be the last thing he'd know before his death.

She jumped to her feet as she heard the jingle of the padlock on the door. Maybe if she rushed him, she could bowl him over and run. She lowered her shoulder and prepared to attack.

The door opened, displaying two things—night had fallen outside, and Jerrod stood before her in the beam of her flashlight with a gun pointed at her chest.

"Don't get any smart ideas, girly," he said. "It doesn't matter to me if I deliver you to Jackson dead or alive."

For a moment she wanted to rush him anyway, let him shoot her now so that Jackson wouldn't have to watch her die. But that tiny survival instinct kicked in, that single ray of hope that somehow, someway, she and Jackson could get out of this together and alive.

"Turn around," he commanded. She hesitated only a moment and then did as he asked. He quickly tied her wrists together and then grabbed hold of her shoulder and spun her around. "Come on, we've got a date. I'll let you sit in the passenger seat as long as you behave, but if you give me any trouble I'll backhand you into unconsciousness. Got it?"

She nodded as he shoved her toward an awaiting SUV. He opened the passenger door and she slid in, wincing at the uncomfortable position of her arms behind her.

He circled the vehicle and slid in behind the steering wheel and started the engine. "This would have all been so much easier if you could hire good help these days. Black had two chances to kill you and he bungled both of them."

"Black? You mean Roger Black?" she asked in stunned surprise.

Jerrod chuckled. "You'd be amazed how easy it is to buy a greedy man."

They hadn't even considered the top-dog deputy as a potential suspect, but then why should they? She knew by Jerrod's answer to her question about Amberly and Cole that he didn't have anything to do with whatever had happened to them.

Jackson's gut instinct that the attacks on them had been personal had been right, and the attacks had nothing to do with the case they'd been investigating.

That meant they had no clues at all about Amberly and Cole's disappearance and moved her closer to believing that somehow the case was related to what Jackson had been working on in Bachelor Moon.

They drove only a short distance and then he stopped the SUV and put it in Park. Every nerve in Marjorie's body went on high alert.

She looked around the area, but still couldn't discern where they were in the darkness of the night. There were no lights to indicate any kind of civilization nearby.

Jerrod pulled a cell phone out of his pocket and flashed Marjorie a smile that was visible in the dashboard illumination. "Time for the games to begin," he said and then punched in a number.

JACKSON HAD DRIVEN up and down each and every street of Mystic Lake, seeking Edward Bentz's van. Not only could he not find it, none of the deputies on duty had managed to locate it, either.

Darkness had fallen and along with it his hope. Maybe this had been his father's intention all along. To take Maggie away from him and place her somewhere that Jackson would never, ever find her again, either dead or alive.

Maybe the true torture was the not knowing what had happened to her…if she was alive, or if she was dead. And if Jerrod had killed her, had she suffered?

He'd been in touch with Deputy Fred Morsi, who was now acting as head deputy, several times through the course of the past couple of hours. Roger was locked up, and although Fred had continued to elicit answers from him, he still swore he had no idea where Jerrod, Edward or Maggie might be.

Jackson was now parked once again in front of the sheriff's station. Night had fallen, and his despair had grown to mammoth proportions as if fed by the darkness itself.

He didn't know where to go. He didn't know what to do. He tasted grief, but refused to acknowledge it. He refused to grieve for Maggie without positive confirmation that she was dead.

He jumped as his cell phone rang. He fumbled it out of his pocket. "Revannaugh," he answered.

"Isn't that a coincidence, it's Revannaugh on this end, too."

The familiar sound of his father's voice churned up a combination of rage and hatred in Jackson that he knew he had to control. "Where is she?"

"The lovely Agent Clinton is right here by my side."

Jackson pressed the phone more tightly against his ear. "If you've hurt her I'll kill you."

Jerrod laughed. "Big talk from a man who doesn't hold the cards."

"What do you want, Jerrod?" Jackson asked the question although he already knew the answer.

"Do you have any idea the indignities I've suffered over the past six years? A man of my stature, in a prison cell with monsters? You put me there, son."

"You put yourself there," Jackson replied.

"You put the final nail in my coffin, my own flesh and blood testifying against me. You want your girlfriend back? Meet me in thirty minutes on the north bank of Mystic Lake, and as they say in the movies, come alone."

"Thirty minutes. I'll be there." Jackson dropped his phone in his pocket, started his car and headed directly toward the lake that was the namesake of the town.

He had no idea what his father intended, had no idea what would go down on the banks of the lake this night. There was a near-full moon that would make it difficult to depend on the darkness of the night for cover.

He had no idea if his father would be alone with Maggie or if Edward Bentz would be with him to provide backup. He didn't even know if Maggie was still alive or if Jerrod intended to deliver her body to his son.

Jackson was certain of just one thing…only one Revannaugh would be leaving the banks of Mystic Lake tonight. Jerrod had pushed him into a corner where he had no options. He would kill his father to save Maggie, and he knew his father would kill him without blinking an eye.

On the north shore of the glittering lake was a thick grove of trees. Jackson pulled into the area and got out of his car, his gun in his hand.

The night was hot, muggy and completely silent, as if Mother Nature knew something bad was coming and had hidden all the insects and night creatures from harm.

Nerves jangled inside him. He waited, unsure from which direction his father would come, uncertain if he might already be here.

He'd been foolish to come without his own backup. He didn't exactly trust the Mystic Lake sheriff's department, given the fact that their top deputy had turned out to be an ineffectual hit man.

He pulled out his phone and dialed the number for Agent Adam Forest. Maggie had given him the number to use in an emergency, and he figured this definitely qualified as an emergency.

It took him only moments to explain the situation with Adam and then hang up. It would be at least twenty to thirty minutes before Adam would arrive, and Jackson was expecting his father within the next ten minutes or so.

Those minutes clicked by in agonizing slowness. During that time, Jackson removed all emotion from his head. He couldn't think of Jerrod as his father and he couldn't think of Maggie as his partner or the woman he loved. The two of them were simply hostage taker and hostage. As long as he thought that way and kept his emotions in check, he would function better in doing whatever needed to be done for a successful outcome.

Despite the heat of the night, Jackson was cool as an unnatural calm descended upon him. He gripped his gun tighter as an SUV approached. The vehicle pulled to a halt, the high-beam lights pointed directly at Jackson, half blinding him.

He squinted and saw a tall man get out of the driver's seat. Jerrod. He held his gun on the man who was his father, but there was no way he would shoot, not without knowing where Maggie was.

He got the answer to that question as Jerrod walked to the passenger side and pulled Maggie out of the car, using her as a shield in front of him as he approached Jackson. He held Maggie with one arm around her neck, and in his other hand was a gun pointed at Jackson.

"Let her go," Jackson said. He kept his gaze on

Jerrod, knowing that one look at Maggie would undo him to the point that he wouldn't be able to function.

"Drop your gun," Jerrod replied.

"You drop yours and let her go. It doesn't have to be this way," Jackson said.

He knew he would shoot Jerrod if he had to, but in a flash, old memories shot through his brain. Jerrod teaching him to ride a bicycle, buying him ice cream and taking him to a movie.

There had been flashes of a father in the monster, but Jackson had never been fooled. He knew exactly what his father was capable of, the kind of man he was at his very core.

"Just let Maggie go and we all walk away from this," he said, although he knew at the very least he'd make sure his father was in custody.

Jerrod laughed, a dry, humorless sound. "Now, we both know you aren't going to just let me walk away from this, and I'm definitely not in the mood to let you walk away. I've had years to think about your betrayal, to wallow in my need to see my own brand of justice served."

He moved the barrel of his gun and pressed it against Maggie's temple. "Maybe if I kill her you'll understand the depth of my unhappiness with you."

For the first time Jackson allowed himself to look at Maggie. He was surprised to see that she appeared calm, as if resigned to whatever happened.

"If you kill her she'll be dead, but then you'll be dead, too," Jackson said, pleased that his voice remained cool and calm.

Jerrod appeared to study him, and once again he moved his gun to point at Jackson. "Then I guess you leave me no choice. I'll just have to kill you first, and then after you are dead I'll take care of your partner."

A shot rang out and Jerrod roared in pain as he dropped his gun, released Maggie and fell to one side on the ground. "You shot me," he screamed at Jackson.

"No, I didn't," Jackson said in bewilderment as Maggie ran to his side.

At that moment, Agent Adam Forest stepped out from behind the SUV. As he walked past the writhing Jerrod, he kicked Jerrod's gun out of reach and smiled.

"I saw an opportunity and so I took it." He looked at Jackson. "No man should have to carry the burden of killing his own father through the rest of his life."

"I'm bleeding to death," Jerrod screamed. "For God's sake, I need help."

Adam returned to the man on the ground and checked out his wound. "Don't be such a baby. It's a clean shot through and through and didn't do any permanent damage." He rose to his feet. "I'll call it in."

Jackson nodded, numbed by the unexpected help. It was only when he grabbed Maggie into his arms that his numbness went away, along with the iciness that had been inside his heart for what felt like days.

He cupped her face, her beautiful face in his hands. "Are you all right? Did he hurt you at all?"

"I'm fine," she assured him. "But I'd love it if you'd unfasten my wrists so I can wrap my arms around you."

He whirled her around and with a pocketknife he sawed through the tape that bound her. She turned around and threw herself at him, her arms wrapping around his neck while her body pressed tightly against his.

"I was so afraid for you," she murmured against his chest.

"I was terrified for you," he replied as he stroked her hair, then caressed her back and breathed in the scent of her.

"I was a little worried myself," Adam said, his voice breaking them apart. "I broke every speed limit to get here and then I was afraid he was going to shoot Jackson before I got a clean shot at his leg."

Jackson looked over to where his father was still on the ground, only now he wore a bracelet of handcuffs. He looked back at Forest. "I don't know how to thank you."

"All in a day's work," Forest replied.

At that moment the sound of sirens rose in the air. "I've got both FBI and local authorities on their way. From what I've heard, Mystic Lake law enforcement is going to need some help getting their stuff together."

As Jackson thought of Roger Black, he nodded his head. "They definitely have some problems." He frowned thoughtfully. "But nothing that went down here tonight had anything to do with the case of Amberly and Cole Caldwell's disappearance."

Maggie moved closer to his side. "At the moment I just want to celebrate the fact that we're both still alive and your father is probably going back to prison for a very long time."

"He'll be facing attempted murder charges, kidnapping and conspiracy—yeah, he won't see the light of day for years to come," Jackson replied.

At that moment a flurry of cars pulled up. Jackson and Maggie were separated as the area swarmed with law enforcement officials. Maggie found herself in the backseat of her director's car.

Daniel Forbes questioned her about not just the events of the night but also what she had known about Jackson's father. She confessed that she'd known nothing about Jerrod Revannnaugh until the moment he'd shown up on her doorstep.

Jerrod had been taken away under armed guard to a hospital to have his wound tended to, then he would be taken to a federal holding cell in Kansas City.

Director Forbes questioned her for a long time, their talk interrupted several times by phone calls he had to take. By the time they were finished, he offered to take her home. Seeing Jackson nowhere in the sea of men and women in the area, she agreed.

When she arrived home, Jackson wasn't there. She went inside, set the security and locked the door and then stumbled to the sofa and collapsed, trying to process everything that had happened, everything that she had learned over the course of the long, tension-filled evening.

It was no wonder Jackson hadn't wanted to talk about his father with her, and it was no wonder that at sixteen Jackson had left his father behind and began to build a different life, a righteous life, for himself.

Thank God Adam had arrived in time to save Jackson the trauma of having to kill…or be killed…by his father. She stood as she heard the sound of a key in the lock, and then Jackson came in. He punched in the code on the keypad, then locked the door behind him and opened his arms to her.

She ran to him, needing to be held, needing to be close to him as the aftermath of the night washed over her. He wrapped her tight in his arms and there were no words necessary as they simply held each other.

She didn't know how long they stood in the embrace, but finally he broke it and led her back to the sofa where they sat side by side.

"I should have told you," he said, his gaze focused on the coffee table. "I should have warned you, but I had no idea that he was plotting against me or that he'd been released from prison."

He finally looked at her, his eyes dark pools of misery. "He was a con man, the kind of man who might have scammed your mother out of any money she possessed. He had married at least six times, and each time he divorced he was wealthier and the woman was destitute. Knowing your history, I never wanted you to know that I got my charm from him. I wasn't sure you'd really believe that that's all I got from him."

"Jackson." She took one of his big hands in hers. "You can't possibly be like your father. If you're a con man you're a very bad one. I don't have any money." She smiled at him teasingly. "That means you've wasted all your charm working it on me."

He gave her a faint smile and pulled his hand from hers. "I've been called back to Baton Rouge."

She looked at him in surprise. "When?"

"I'm on a ten o'clock flight tomorrow."

"But we haven't solved the crime. We still have people missing," she protested.

"I think the powers that be have decided that the two cases might possibly be linked. The Kansas City FBI will continue to follow up here, but I'm heading home tomorrow."

And now the heartache begins, she thought as pain

pierced through her. Tomorrow she would no longer have him in her life. Tomorrow he would be back in Baton Rouge, charming the ladies, and in no time at all he'd forget all about her.

"I hate to see you go," she said softly.

"Then come with me." He grabbed her hands and pulled her closer to him. "I'm sure you're due some time off. If I was to guess, you haven't taken a real vacation since you started the job. Come with me, Maggie. Let me show you my city, let me show you how much I love you."

She stared at his face, expecting to see a teasing twinkle in his eyes, an indication that he was joking, but there was only love and want in the depths of his eyes.

"I love you, Maggie. I love you like I've never loved anyone else in my life. I want to give to you, to make you happy. Come visit and let's see where this all goes. You can get a transfer and we can buy a big place with a carriage-house apartment for your mother."

Marjorie pulled her hands from his. Wasn't this what she'd wanted? For him to love her as much as she loved him? And yet it all seemed too fast. Her head was spinning. Things were going far too fast.

"Jackson, I…I don't know what to say."

He stared at her for a long moment. "I'd say that says it all," he replied as shutters fell over his eyes. He stood. "I'd better get packed up. I'll need to be at the airport by eight-thirty or so. You want to drive me or should I arrange for a cab?"

"Of course I'll drive you," she said.

"Then I'll see you in the morning." He turned and went into his bedroom and closed the door behind him.

She remained seated on the sofa, a million words unsaid, a thousand regrets already forming. But it was crazy to believe that they could build a life together. They weren't meant to be, they'd never been meant to be anything more than partners.

She wasn't his Maggie, she was Marjorie Clinton, a Kansas City FBI agent who was good at her job and didn't take chances in her personal life.

THE RIDE TO THE AIRPORT the next morning was silent and awkward. Jackson knew Maggie loved him. She'd told him how she felt about him, that he'd managed to get deep into her heart, and yet not so deep that she wanted to take it any further.

It was a bitch, that the first woman Jackson had fallen in love with apparently wasn't as deeply in love with him. First love, first heartbreak. He hadn't expected either of them. But then, he hadn't expected Maggie.

When they reached Terminal A, she circled around to the drop-off area and halted the car. She got out of the driver's seat as he got out and retrieved his duffel bag from the backseat.

She joined him on the curb. She was dressed in a yellow blouse, which enhanced the beauty of her red-gold hair, and the pair of black jeans he'd bought when they'd been at the hotel. She was an ache inside him.

"Then I guess this is goodbye," she said. "You have your ticket and your boarding pass?"

"I have everything I need," he replied. *Except you.* "Goodbye, Maggie." Before he could stop his impulse, he dropped the duffel to the ground, pulled her into his arms and kissed her with all the love, all the emotion that was in his heart, in his soul.

When he released her, he didn't look at her again. He grabbed his duffel and went through the doors that would take him into the terminal.

He found his gate and passed through security easily, then sank down on one of the padded chairs to wait the hour and a half for his flight.

Maybe he'd pushed too hard. There was no question in his mind that Maggie loved him. And now there were no more secrets between them. She knew about his father and had judged him as his own man, not for his father's sins.

Maybe he should have told his director he needed a little downtime, hung around here and allowed their love to grow a bit more before encouraging her to leave everything behind and come with him to Baton Rouge.

He knew Maggie. He knew the kind of woman she was, and he'd been wrong to press her so aggressively. Maybe the best thing to do was to cancel his ticket home and pursue the woman who was the love of his life.

He stood from his seat at the same time Maggie came running toward him. He stared at her in surprise. "I have a ticket," she said. "I'm going with you." She laughed in carefree abandon. "I don't have any clothes, I don't even have a toothbrush, but I'm not letting you leave without me."

Still stunned, he fell back into his chair. "I was just about to go cancel my ticket," he said. "I didn't want to leave you. What changed your mind?"

She sank down into the chair next to his. "The whole time I was locked up in that shed waiting to find out if your father was going to kill me, I had a thousand regrets, and one of those regrets was that I hadn't taken more chances in my personal life."

She reached for his hand. "I'm taking a chance now, Jackson. I'm taking a chance on you...on us. I love you and I want to see if we can make this work. I need a man who brings me laughter, whose kisses make me weak in the knees. I need a charmer who flirts with his eyes and has a smile that melts my heart."

"And that would be me," he said.

He stood and pulled her up and into his arms. As he kissed her once again, she knew in the very core of her being that they were meant to be together, that somehow, someway, this magic between them was going to last a lifetime. Primal energy, that was what Natalie Redwing had called it, but in truth it was simply love.

Epilogue

Amberly Caldwell woke to small fingers stroking the long length of her dark hair.

"Macy, stop bothering Amberly." Daniella's voice came from nearby.

"I just wish sometimes that I had long pretty black hair," Macy's childish voice said.

Amberly turned over on the small bunk where she'd slept and faced the little blond-haired girl, who was on a bunk next to her. Iron bars separated the two beds. She smiled at Macy. "There were lots of times when I was little that I wished I had pretty blond curls just like yours."

She reached through the bars and gave Macy's slender shoulder a gentle squeeze and tried not to think of her son, Max.

Cole was already awake and out of his top bunk. He and Sam Connelly stood at the back end of the prison-like cells they were each held in, talking through the bars in low whispers.

Each cell was identical, with bunk beds built into the steel, a stall shower and prisonlike stool and a curtain that could be pulled around the bathroom area for a bit of privacy.

She and Cole occupied one cell, and Daniella, Sam and little Macy occupied the one next to them. None of them knew where they were or why they had been taken from their homes and brought here.

Sam and Daniella had lost track of the time they'd been held captive, and although Amberly knew it had been a couple of weeks since she and Cole had been brought here from his home, she didn't know specifically how many days it had been.

All she knew for certain was they were in trouble. Twice a day a man clad in black and wearing a ski mask brought them trays of food, but he'd never spoken to any of them.

The men had finally stopped asking questions. "A waste of breath," Sam had said. "He'll tell us what's going on when he's ready, but he obviously isn't going to be goaded into speaking before then."

The men had already searched the cells for any weakness, they'd tried to figure out escape plans, but none appeared to be viable. The only way in and out of the cells was through the locked doors, and since their arrival the doors had never been unlocked.

The food trays were slid through a slot without the need for their captor to open the doors. The only thing she knew about the man who held them was that his eyes were the coldest ice-blue that she'd ever seen.

They had speculated on why they had been kidnapped, why they were being held, but nobody had come up with any viable answers.

The only small sense of relief she had was the fact that none of them had seen his face, none of them had heard his voice. There was no way any of them could identify him, and as long as that remained true, they had a chance for surviving whatever plot was in progress.

But Amberly knew that the minute he came without his ski mask on and they saw his face, none of them would leave this place, wherever it was, alive.

* * * * *

Don't miss the continuation of Carla's series,
coming to you later in 2014
from Harlequin Intrigue!

REQUEST YOUR FREE BOOKS!
2 FREE NOVELS PLUS 2 FREE GIFTS!

H HARLEQUIN®

INTRIGUE®

BREATHTAKING ROMANTIC SUSPENSE

YES! Please send me 2 FREE Harlequin Intrigue® novels and my 2 FREE gifts (gifts are worth about $10). After receiving them, if I don't wish to receive any more books, I can return the shipping statement marked "cancel." If I don't cancel, I will receive 6 brand-new novels every month and be billed just $4.74 per book in the U.S. or $5.24 per book in Canada. That's a savings of at least 14% off the cover price! It's quite a bargain! Shipping and handling is just 50¢ per book in the U.S. and 75¢ per book in Canada.* I understand that accepting the 2 free books and gifts places me under no obligation to buy anything. I can always return a shipment and cancel at any time. Even if I never buy another book, the two free books and gifts are mine to keep forever.

182/382 HDN F42N

Name	(PLEASE PRINT)	
Address		Apt. #
City	State/Prov.	Zip/Postal Code

Signature (if under 18, a parent or guardian must sign)

Mail to the **Harlequin® Reader Service:**
IN U.S.A.: P.O. Box 1867, Buffalo, NY 14240-1867
IN CANADA: P.O. Box 609, Fort Erie, Ontario L2A 5X3
**Are you a subscriber to Harlequin Intrigue books
and want to receive the larger-print edition?
Call 1-800-873-8635 or visit www.ReaderService.com.**

* Terms and prices subject to change without notice. Prices do not include applicable taxes. Sales tax applicable in N.Y. Canadian residents will be charged applicable taxes. Offer not valid in Quebec. This offer is limited to one order per household. Not valid for current subscribers to Harlequin Intrigue books. All orders subject to credit approval. Credit or debit balances in a customer's account(s) may be offset by any other outstanding balance owed by or to the customer. Please allow 4 to 6 weeks for delivery. Offer available while quantities last.

Your Privacy—The Harlequin® Reader Service is committed to protecting your privacy. Our Privacy Policy is available online at www.ReaderService.com or upon request from the Harlequin Reader Service.

We make a portion of our mailing list available to reputable third parties that offer products we believe may interest you. If you prefer that we not exchange your name with third parties, or if you wish to clarify or modify your communication preferences, please visit us at www.ReaderService.com/consumerchoice or write to us at Harlequin Reader Service Preference Service, P.O. Box 9062, Buffalo, NY 14269. Include your complete name and address.

HI13R

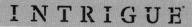
Hayes stepped out into the cool night air and took a deep breath of
Montana. The night was dark, and yet he could still see the outline of
the mountains that surrounded the valley.

Maybe he would drive on up the canyon tonight after all, he thought.
It was such a beautiful June night, and he didn't feel as tired as he had
earlier. He'd eat the sandwich on his way and—

As he started toward his rented SUV parked by itself in the large
lot, he saw a man toss what looked like a bright-colored shoe into his
trunk before struggling to pick up a woman from the pavement between
a large, dark car and a lighter-colored SUV. Both were parked some
distance away from his vehicle in an unlit part of the lot.

Had the woman fallen? Was she hurt?

As the man lifted the woman, Hayes realized that the man was about
to put her into the trunk of the car.

What the hell?

"Hey!" he yelled.

The man turned in surprise. Hayes only got a fleeting impression of
the man, since he was wearing a baseball cap pulled low and his face
was in shadow in the dark part of the lot.

"Hey!" Hayes yelled again as he dropped his groceries. The wine
hit the pavement and exploded, but Hayes paid no attention as he raced
toward the man.

The man seemed to panic, stumbling over a bag of groceries on the ground under him. He fell to one knee and dropped the woman again to the pavement. Struggling to his feet, he left the woman where she was and rushed around to the driver's side of the car.

As Hayes sprinted toward the injured woman, the man leaped behind the wheel, started the car and sped off.

Hayes tried to get a license plate, but it was too dark. He rushed to the woman on the ground. She hadn't moved. As he dropped to his knees next to her, the car roared out of the grocery parking lot and disappeared down the highway. He'd only gotten an impression of the make of the vehicle and even less of a description of the man.

As dark as it was, though, he could see that the woman was bleeding from a cut on the side of her face. He felt for a pulse, then dug out his cell phone and called for the police and an ambulance.

Waiting for 911 to answer, he noticed that the woman was missing one of her bright red high-heeled shoes. The operator answered and he quickly gave her the information. As he disconnected he looked down to see that the woman's eyes had opened. A sea of blue-green peered up at him. He felt a small chill ripple through him before he found his voice. "You're going to be all right. You're safe now."

The eyes blinked then closed.

Can he protect her from a danger that's much closer than they think…a killer hiding in plain sight who's about to spring a final trap?

Find out what happens next in
RESCUE AT CARDWELL RANCH
by NEW YORK TIMES *bestselling author B.J. Daniels,*
available June 2014, only from Harlequin® Intrigue®.

HIEXP69764

HARLEQUIN®

A *Romance* FOR EVERY MOOD™

Love the Harlequin book you just read?

Your opinion matters.

Review this book on your favorite
book site, review site, blog or your own
social media properties and share
your opinion with other readers!

Be sure to connect with us at:
Harlequin.com/Newsletters
Facebook.com/HarlequinBooks
Twitter.com/HarlequinBooks